Sophie C. Durand

Napoleon and Marie-Louise

1810-1814 - A Memoir

Sophie C. Durand

Napoleon and Marie-Louise
1810-1814 - A Memoir

ISBN/EAN: 9783337349974

Printed in Europe, USA, Canada, Australia, Japan

Cover: Foto ©Andreas Hilbeck / pixelio.de

More available books at **www.hansebooks.com**

NAPOLEON AND MARIE-LOUISE

1810—1814

A MEMOIR

BY

MADAME LA GÉNÉRALE DURAND

FIRST LADY TO THE EMPRESS MARIE-LOUISE

LONDON

SAMPSON LOW, MARSTON, SEARLE & RIVINGTON

CROWN BUILDINGS, 188, FLEET STREET

1886

LONDON :
PRINTED BY WILLIAM CLOWES AND SONS, LIMITED,
STAMFORD STREET AND CHARING CROSS.

PREFACE TO THE FIRST EDITION,
PUBLISHED IN 1819.

It is right that I should give to the public certain details regarding a work in which many persons still living figure unfavourably. It is much against my will that I find myself obliged to give these reminiscences prominence which I did not intend for them. After the departure of the Empress Marie-Louise, in whose service I was for four years, I was desirous of collecting the various notes which I had made, under the name of Souvenirs. I retraced all that I had seen, the anecdotes to whose authenticity I was a witness, those which had been related to me, and which I had verified; I depicted the illustrious persons whom I served with the sentiments of gratitude and respect due to them. I was far indeed from insulting him whose misfortunes have been so great—that is a baseness of which I am incapable.

I had sketched out their portraits, all prompted by truth, but without any reflections, and especially without any evil speaking.

A friend of my family, who has been living for some time in London, wrote to me a year ago, that he had collected a great deal of material, and was about to publish memorials of Napoleon and his family. He begged me to communicate to him the notes which he knew I possessed. Either from a presentiment or from prudence, I at first refused on the score of the many sorrows of my life, and my fear of reviving them by such publicity. He re-assured me by protesting that he would conceal my identity. Yielding to his renewed importunities, I sent him the memoranda for which he had asked. But what was my astonishment when several persons spoke to me of a pamphlet which had arrived from London, in which the Court of Napoleon was most severely handled. Although the work was forbidden, I succeeded in procuring a copy, and found in it a portion of the notes and portraits that I had sent, but totally disfigured by reflections as ill-placed as they were improper. The author, finding my portraits insipid, wanted to render them piquant. He did not perceive that he made them odious. To these portraits are added unfounded anecdotes, which I owe it to the truth to deny, all the more that the author, in a preface which he had no right whatever to place at the head of his book, has almost pointed me out as the writer of it.

I submit these Souvenirs to the public, just as I wrote them for my own family, and I give my name, because, if this work be worthy of blame, that blame should fall only upon myself, and not upon estimable persons who have been very unjustly accused.*

* This final edition of the "Mémoires sur Napoléon et Marie-Louise" had been prepared by Madame la Générale Durand, who died without having published them.

They could not have been placed before the public at an earlier date.—Editor's Note.

CONTENTS.

CHAPTER I.

CHAPTER II.

CHAPTER III.

NAPOLEON.

CHAPTER IV.

CHAPTER V.

CHAPTER VI.

CHAPTER VII.

CHAPTER VIII.

CHAPTER IX.

CHAPTER X.

CHAPTER XV.

NAPOLEON AT FONTAINEBLEAU.

CHAPTER XVI.

CHAPTER XVII.

CHAPTER XVIII.

NAPOLEON AND MARIE-LOUISE.

CHAPTER I.

THE FAMILY OF NAPOLEON—JEROME, KING OF WESTPHALIA—THE
PRINCESS OF WÜRTEMBURG—THE DUC D'ENGHIEN—CAUSE OF THE
DIVORCE OF NAPOLEON AND JOSEPHINE—MARIE-LOUISE.

It was the end of 1809. The fresh victories just won
by the Emperor had rendered his crown secure; his
glory was complete, but for his ambition and his
happiness an heir was needed. He could not hope
for issue of his marriage with Josephine, and death
had recently removed the eldest son of his brother
Louis. The child had been generally regarded as his
uncle's successor; some people went so far, indeed, as
to assert that he was his son, and that the Emperor
had given Hortense Beauharnais in marriage to Louis,
solely in order to conceal the result of his own relations with her. In support of what, after all, could be
no more than a conjecture, it was said that Louis
never could endure his wife, and thus it is that truth
sometimes serves to propagate falsehood. It is certain

B

that Napoleon never was unduly intimate with Hortense, but that he loved her as he loved her brother Eugene, because the two were the children of his wife.

In the various marriages which he decreed, whether in his own family or among the personages of his Court, he never consulted inclination; he listened to nothing except convenience. His will was an absolute command: this was proved in the case of his brother Jerome, who, having married Miss Patterson in America, without his consent, was forced to abandon his wife and child and to marry the Princess of Wurtemburg. It is said that for a long time the marriage was a nominal one, and indeed, that the King had vowed he would never have any relations with a wife who had been thus forced upon him. For three years he lavished his attentions upon almost all the beauties of the Westphalian Court. The Queen, an eye-witness of this conduct, bore it with mild and forbearing dignity; she seemed to see and hear nothing; in short, her demeanour was perfect. The King, touched by her goodness, weary of his conquests, and repentant of his behaviour, was only anxious for an opportunity of altering the state of things. Happily, the propitious moment presented itself. The right wing of the Palace at Cassel, in which the Queen's apartments were situated, took fire; alarmed by the screams of her women, the Queen awoke and sprang out of her bed, to be caught in the arms of the King, and carried to a place of safety. From that time forth the royal

couple were united and happy. The Queen was pregnant when she lost the throne, and never was there a
woman who behaved more nobly than she did to her
husband, who, homeless and proscribed, found rank
and fortune in the realm of his father-in-law: these
he owed to the affection of his wife, who never would
abandon him.

Louis was also obliged to submit to the absolute
will of the Emperor, who insisted on his marrying
Hortense Beauharnais, notwithstanding his attachment to another person. Hence the indifference of
Louis to his wife. And yet Hortense was handsome,
graceful, gifted with many talents, and one who might
well have won a husband's love. She had three
children by Louis; the first and second are dead; the
only one remaining of that family is Prince Louis
Napoleon, who was born in 1808. Hortense made
many strenuous efforts to win her husband's heart, but
all in vain. Nor did Louis ever forgive his brother
for the violence that had been done to his inclinations.
Dissension reigned between them from that time forth,
and when, after the death of the eldest son of Louis
and Hortense, the Emperor asked him for the second
in order that he might adopt him, Louis positively
refused. The second boy died in Italy; Prince
Louis is the third son of the King and Queen of
Holland.

Napoleon, who aspired to the glory of being the
founder of a fourth dynasty, wanted, nevertheless, an

heir, and an heir whom he might form betimes to his own maxims. From this time forth he caused his divorce to be talked of; he took care to let the idea spread without contradiction, and he saw that he might safely take that step whenever it should appear good in his eyes, without hurting the feelings of his subjects too keenly. Josephine disputed the ground with him for some time. She was universally liked; she had as much ascendency over him as it was possible for any one to obtain; she was besides so graceful and amiable, she was so well versed in all the arts of pleasing, that she diverted many a storm; and she alone had the gift of soothing a naturally imperious and irascible temper.

When Bonaparte, then First Consul, desired to make himself Emperor, he encountered serious resistance in his own family. His mother and his brother Lucien made great efforts to induce him to renounce the idea, but in vain. The conflict ended. Madame Lætitia and Lucien left France for Rome, from whence Lucien never returned until the Hundred Days.

The opposition of his family troubled the First Consul but little; that which he had to encounter from the Jacobin and Republican parties was much more serious. The name of king or emperor was odious to both. They were still attached to that phantom of Equality to which they had raised altars. They dared not, however, say openly that they refused Bonaparte for a sovereign, and, while they hated him they lavished adulation upon him. They pretended to believe that his only design in restoring the throne was to pave the way for the re-establishment of the Bourbon, and to act in France the part which Monk had played in England, and to this pretext they assigned their obstinate resistance.

Cambacérès and Fouché, who were specially charged with the smoothing of the path by which the First Consul was to reach the throne, made known to him the fear and suspicion to which his project had given rise. They added that the Royalists were conspiring in the dark, that the police were aware of this, but had not yet got hold of all the threads of the plot, which they would need to enable them to act with safety. A few days later, it was known that an individual, who was treated with great observance and respect, had had an interview with General Moreau. Fouché assured the First Consul that the personage was a prince of the house of Bourbon. The First Consul doubted this: he knew that the Dukes of Berry and Angoulême were in England; he knew also that the Duke of Enghien had gone to the play at Strasburg several times, and returned the following day to Etenheim. Nevertheless, he was told over and over again that a conspiracy against him was being organized, and that the confederates prided themselves upon having a prince at their head.

The personage who had held the reported conferences with Moreau had escaped arrest. All the

information which Bonaparte received tended to make
him resolve upon having the Duke of Enghien seized.
The Prince was taken to Versailles, tried, and shot
in the night.   There is a mystery in this matter,*
for the First Consul directed State-Councillor Réal to
go to Vincennes and bring the judgment to him.
It was late when M. Réal left Saint Cloud ; he went
from thence to his own house, and when he arrived
at Vincennes in the morning, all was over.

The death of the Duke of Enghien was an addition-
ally deplorable crime, in that he was innocent, and
the trial of George proved that Pichegru had been
taken for the Prince.

So firmly convinced was the Duke of Bourbon
that he owed the death of his son to Fouché and
Talleyrand, that he never would go to the Court of
the Restoration while they were there.

Once seated on the throne, the Emperor sought
for the means of providing himself with an heir.
There was no hope of his wife's giving him a son,
and thenceforth the idea of divorce was constantly
present to him.   Josephine dreaded, and did all in
her power to avert, her fate ; but fortune had decreed
her fall, and it was hastened by some differences which
occurred between the Emperor and herself.   Four
months afterwards the divorce took place.

* The mystery is dispelled by the "Memoirs of Madame de
Rémusat," and an extraordinary contribution by M. Fauriel to the
history of the period, entitled "The Last Days of the Consulate."
(Sampson Low and Co.)—Translator's note.

No sooner was the deed done, than all Europe
fixed its eyes on France, and a thousand conjectures
were formed as to the princess who should be chosen
as consort of the sovereign. Savary, Duke of Rovigo, was despatched to Russia to ask for the hand
of a sister of the Czar Alexander. The negotiation
appeared to be on the point of succeeding when the
Empress-mother asked for time before she gave her
consent. This adjournment was regarded as a refusal,
and Austria having offered Marie-Louise, she was
accepted. The public was still seeking among the
various courts of Europe the Princess destined to
wear the crown-matrimonial of France, when they
learned that Napoleon had won one of whom they had
never thought, a Princess of the Imperial house of
Austria, a grandniece of Marie-Antoinette.

When the Duke of Vicenza, our ambassador at
St. Petersburg, waited upon the Empress-mother to
announce to her the marriage of Napoleon, she
thought he had come to receive her own reply, and
hastened to tell him that she accorded her daughter
to his master. The Duke, greatly surprised, was
obliged to explain to the Empress that her postponement
having been taken for a refusal, the offer of Austria
had been accepted, and that his mission was to announce
the marriage of Marie-Louise with his sovereign.

Berthier, Prince of Neufchatel, received the nuptial
benediction at Vienna, as proxy for the Emperor, and
the Strasburg road was speedily thronged with equi-

pages conveying the household of the new Empress to
Brannau, where she was to dismiss her own suite.

Marie-Louise was then eighteen years and a half
old; she had a majestic figure, a noble carriage, a great
deal of freshness and bloom, fair hair which was not
insipid, blue eyes, but they had animation in them,
hands and feet which might have served as models for
a sculptor. She was, perhaps, a little too stout—a
defect she soon got rid of in France. Such were the
personal advantages which were first remarked in her.
Nothing could be more gracious, more amiable than
her face, when she was quite at ease, either in her
private life or in the society of those persons with
whom she was particularly intimate; but in public,
and especially on her first arrival in France, her
timidity gave her an embarrassed air which many
people mistook for haughtiness.

She had been very carefully educated; her tastes
were simple, her mind was cultivated, she expressed
herself in French with facility, indeed with as much
ease as in her mother tongue. She was calm, reflec-
tive, kindly, and feeling-hearted, although not demon-
strative; she had all the feminine accomplishments,
loved occupation, and did not know the meaning of
ennui. No woman could have suited Napoleon
better. Gentle, peaceable, a stranger to every kind
of intrigue, she never meddled in public affairs, and
indeed most frequently derived her knowledge of
them from the newspapers. To crown the happiness

of the Emperor, it pleased Providence that this young
Princess, who might have regarded him only as the
persecutor of her family, the man who had twice
obliged them to fly from Vienna, was delighted to be
able to captivate him in whom fame acclaimed the
hero of Europe, and soon came to regard him with
the most tender affection.

CHAPTER II.

AMONG the number of persons awaiting the new Empress at Brannau, there were several who had known Marie-Antoinette. All these pictured to themselves what must be the feelings of Marie-Louise on coming to seat herself upon the throne which had brought such misfortune to her grand-aunt.

The Princess arrived: there was nothing sad in her bearing; she was gracious to all, and had the faculty of pleasing almost everybody. She did not part with the persons who had accompanied her from Vienna without emotion, but she bore the separation with courage. At the moment when she stepped into the carriage that was to take her to Munich, the Grand Master of her household, an old man of sixty-five, who had come thus far with her, raised his clasped hands to Heaven, as if imploring Providence on behalf of his young mistress, and blessing her like a father. His eyes revealed a soul full of great thoughts and sad recollections; his tears drew answering tears from the witnesses of this touching scene. Of all her Austrian suite, her Grand Mistress, Madame Lajenski, who had been permitted to accompany her to Paris, was the only one that remained with her. She set out with her new household without knowing a single person among those who formed it.

Here I must briefly explain the composition of that household. The Princess Caroline, Madame Murat, then Queen of Naples, the Emperor's sister, had been charged with the arrangement of it, and she had come to Brannau to receive her sister-in-law. The Duchess of Montebello, handsome, prudent, the mother of five children, and who had lost her husband in the last battle, had been appointed Lady-in-Waiting (or "of honour"), a poor compensation offered to her by the Emperor for the loss of her husband. The Countess of Luçay, a gentle, good woman, with perfect manners, and who was familiar with the great world, was her Lady of the Bedchamber. I shall speak hereafter of the Ladies of the Palace, whose functions, entirely ruled by etiquette, rarely brought them into personal relations with the Empress, but each of whom had, nevertheless, her pretensions, which were injured by the presence of Madame de Lajenski. The complaints they made to Queen Caroline induced her to commit an act of despotism by which her sister-in-law was deeply hurt.

The object of Madame Murat's ambition was to acquire a great ascendency over Marie-Louise, and if she had acted more adroitly she might have attained it. M. de Talleyrand said of her that she had the head of Cromwell on the body of a pretty woman. She had by nature a striking character, fine intelligence, great ideas, quick and supple wit, grace, and amiability; what she lacked was the art of hiding her love of domination; and when she did not attain her object, it was because she tried to reach it too quickly. From the moment at which she first saw the Princess, she believed herself to have divined her character, and she was completely mistaken. She took her timidity for weakness, her embarrassment for awkwardness; she thought she had nothing to do but command, and she closed against her for ever the heart which she had aspired to rule.

The presence of Madame de Lajenski had excited the jealousy and the fears of almost all the ladies of the Empress's household. They intrigued, they caballed, they told the Queen of Naples that she would never have either the confidence or the affection of her sister-in-law, so long as she kept a person near her who had all the advantage of years of services bestowed and intimacy fostered. The Lady of Honour complained that her functions would be reduced to nothing if the Empress had with her a foreigner who would be all-in-all to her. At last they induced the Queen to demand of Marie-Louise that she should dismiss

Madame Lajenski, although a promise had been made
that she should remain in France for a year. The
Princess, who sincerely desired to gain the affection
of the persons with whom she would have to live,
made no resistance, and Madame de Lajenski returned
to Vienna, taking with her a little dog belonging to
Marie-Louise. She was required to deprive herself of
this dumb friend also on the pretext that the Emperor
had frequently complained of Josephine's dogs. The
Princess made these sacrifices with fortitude; the
odium of them fell upon the Queen of Naples.

But Madame Murat did even worse than this:
after she had exacted the Empress's consent to the
departure of Madame Lajenski, she gave orders to the
ladies in attendance to prevent the former *Grande
Maîtresse* from entering the presence of Marie-Louise
if she should come to take leave. This command was
not obeyed; the ladies, shocked at such harshness,
brought Madame Lajenski in by a back door; she
passed two hours with her former pupil, and notwithstanding the reprimand which their conduct brought
down on them from the Queen, they never repented
of it.

The Empress travelled by easy stages, and a fête
was prepared at each town through which she passed.
At Munich, a letter from the Emperor was handed to
her, and arrangements had been made that one (brought
from Paris by a page) should greet her each morning when she rose. She wrote a reply before she

resumed her journey, and a page started off for the capital with the missive. This epistolary interchange lasted during the entire journey, that is to say, fifteen days, and it was remarked that Marie-Louise perused the letters that were brought to her with growing interest. The Emperor's handwriting was very diffi- cult to read. The Duchess had often seen it in her husband's hands; she helped Marie-Louise to decipher Napoleon's billets-doux, and the intimacy and confi- dence which arose from this were probably the cause of the Empress's strong attachment to her Lady-in- Waiting. She was always eager for these letters, and if the courier happened to be detained by any cause, she would ask over and over again whether he had not yet arrived, and what could have occurred to cause the delay. We must conclude that the corre- spondence was of a very charming nature, since it had already given birth to a sentiment which soon acquired great strength.

Napoleon, on his part, was extremely eager to behold his young bride; this marriage was more flattering to his vanity than the conquest of an empire would have been. He was particularly delighted because he knew that Marie-Louise had voluntarily consented, and not merely as a princess who sacrifices herself to great political interests. Several times he was heard to curse the ceremonial and the fêtes that retarded the much-desired interview, which was to take place at Soissons, where a camp had been formed for the reception of the Empress. Unable to control his impatience, the Emperor repaired thither twenty-four hours before the arrival of the Princess, and so soon as he learned that she was within ten leagues, he set off with the King of Naples to meet her. The two carriages encountered each other at four leagues distance from Soissons; the Emperor got out of his, opened the door of the Empress's, and rather flung himself into than entered it. The Prince of Neuf-chatel had given Marie-Louise a portrait of Napoleon, and she had so often looked at it that his features were familiar to her. Murat had also got into the carriage, and the two married couples regarded each other for a few moments in silence. This the Empress was the first to break, and she said in a tone very complimentary to the Emperor, "Sire, your portrait is not flattered."

It was, however; but love was already exercising its sweet influence, and she looked at the Emperor with eyes prejudiced in his favour. Napoleon was charmed with her; indeed, such was his enthusiasm that he stopped at Soissons, where they were to have remained until the next day, for a few minutes only, and then went on at once to Compiègne. It appears that the entreaties of Napoleon and the urgency of Queen Caroline prevailed with Marie-Louise, and that she did not insist on denying her too happy bride-groom the privileges of a husband until after the religious marriage.

CHAPTER III.

NAPOLEON.

CEREMONY OF THE RELIGIOUS MARRIAGE—THE EMPEROR'S LIFE—HIS
PRIVATE HABITS—HIS PUBLIC BEHAVIOUR—HIS CHARACTER—TRAITS
OF KINDNESS AND BENEFICENCE.

EVERYBODY has read the details of the ceremony of
the religious marriage of the Emperor and Empress.
The great gallery of the Louvre, splendidly decorated,
and furnished with six rows of benches on each side,
was occupied by richly dressed women : at the end
was the temporary chapel in which the clergy awaited
the bridal pair.   The Emperor, on his arrival, took the
Empress by the hand.   Her train was borne by four
queens, those of Naples, Spain, Holland, and Wurtemburg, followed by the kings, and the great officers of
the Crown.   It was a magnificent spectacle for the
public.

We, who were behind the scenes, had one of a
different sort.   The Emperor was a long time before he
could settle himself comfortably into his gorgeous
Spanish costume of white satin, embroidered in gold,

with a mantle of the same covered with golden bees. He found his black velvet cap, adorned with eight rows of diamonds, and three white plumes fastened by a knot, with the regent blazing in the centre of it, particularly troublesome. This splendid headgear was put on and taken off several times, and we tried many different ways of placing it before we succeeded. In spite of ourselves, we were obliged to laugh at the awkward attempts of the kings to drape themselves gracefully in their mantles. The four queens condemned to carry the mantle of the Empress were very much annoyed, and, notwithstanding our advice, did it extremely ill.* We were substituted for them so far as the entrance to the great gallery, and at that point they replaced us.

In this place I must draw the portrait of Napoleon. He was then forty-one years old. In his youth he was very thin, and had a greenish-olive complexion, a long face, and dull eyes; his whole physiognomy was anything rather than agreeable.

In camp, and during his early campaigns, Napoleon feared no fatigue, braved the worst weather, slept under a wretched tent, and seemed to forget all care for his person. In his palace he bathed almost every day, rubbed his whole body over with eau de Cologne, and sometimes changed his linen several times in the

* See Madame de Rémusat's account of the conduct of Napoleon's sisters at the coronation of the Emperor and Josephine. For the proper appreciation of this scene it must be borne in mind that the Queen of Holland was Josephine's daughter.—Translator's note.

day. His favourite costume was that of the mounted
Chasseurs de la Garde. When travelling, he did not
care what sort of lodging he had, provided that no ray
of light could get into his bedroom; he could not bear
even a night-lamp. His table was supplied with the
daintiest dishes; but he never touched them. His
favourite fare was grilled breast of mutton, or a roast
fowl, with lentils or haricot beans. He was very particular about the quality of bread, and he drank none
but the best wine, and very little of it. It has been
stated that he drank eight or ten cups of coffee daily;
but this is a fable, to be discarded with so many
others. He took a small cup of coffee after his breakfast, and the same after his dinner. It is true, he was
so absent and preoccupied, that it has occasionally
happened to him to ask for his coffee immediately
after he had drank it, and to persist in asserting that
he had not taken it. He ate very fast, and rose the
moment he had done, without troubling himself as to
whether those who were admitted to his table had
had time to dine. It has also been asserted that he
took the greatest precautions against poison; this,
too, is a pure falsehood. Perhaps he was too careless
in that respect. Every morning his breakfast was
brought up to an ante-room to which all persons who
had obtained an audience-order had access, and
where they had to wait, sometimes, long enough. The
dishes, which were kept warm, were frequently left
there for several hours until orders were given for the

meal to be served. Dinner was brought in by servants, in covered baskets; but nothing in the world could have been easier than to slip poison into the food if anybody had wanted to do so.

He spoke in a loud voice, and when he was in a merry mood his peals of laughter could be heard from afar. He was fond of singing, although he had a bad voice, and never could sing an air in tune. He took particular pleasure in singing " Ah! c'en est fait, je me marie," or " Si le roi m'avait donné Paris, sa grand ville."

Every year he regulated his household " budget," having statements of the expenditure in each department laid before him, and discussing the items. When he had arrived at the total, he struck off twenty, thirty, or forty thousand francs from the lump sum, saying this was enough, and that the household must be maintained on what he gave. In vain did the Grand Marshal, the Master of the Horse, the Grand Huntsman, the Grand Chamberlain complain and make representations; all was useless, and, as a matter of fact, nothing was worse done in consequence.

The Emperor had the same way of dealing with his Ministers; he retrenched and suppressed in detail, and when the budget was finally drawn up, he again reduced it by one-fourth or one-sixth. They grumbled, and declared that the public service suffered; he merely laughed at them, and that was all they gained by their complaints. Being forced to

economize, each man busied himself with his own
department, and ended by finding that he could do
with the allotted sum.

Those who have lived in close contact with the
Emperor know that he possessed tact and perception,
that he knew how to manage and use men. To this
talent he owed his power. It has been said that he
despised everybody about him ; I do not know whether
that is true or not, but it is of my own knowledge
that he was cold and polite to those whom he did not
like, and that he said harsh and unpleasant things
only to those whom he did like. He did not, however, carry this to the extent of using expressions of
contempt. I can confidently assert that the sayings
which certain pamphlets impute to him were never
uttered by him. He did not say that the Chamberlains
were footmen, with only the difference that they wore
red livery instead of green. It is equally false that
he said he liked Savary because he would kill his own
father if he (the Emperor) ordered him to do so. No
sensible person would believe so atrocious an absurdity. Numbers of people nowadays * are eager to run
down Napoleon. I am convinced that those who now
cry out against him most loudly, are the same who
flattered him most egregiously. There are so many
who want to have it forgotten that but for him they
would have remained in the lowest classes of society
but they are mistaken ; the noise they make merely

* 1819.

evokes recollections anything but favourable to themselves. Napoleon had faults enough without their
being invented for him; nor can any defame him
without insulting the nation whose head he was for
ten years, and also the sovereigns who allied themselves with him.

I have spoken already of his perception and quick-
ness: I will now add that he had a great deal of
general information upon all subjects; he was not a
stranger to any art; he loved letters, and appreciated
learned men; he had singled out and attached to
his person (as Grand Master of Ceremonies) Count de
Ségur, whose wit, amiability, and songs were talked of
long before he was known as the author of those
works which have raised him to a high place among
men of letters. His family, also, in which talent
seems to be hereditary, was well placed at Court. The
Count was an accomplished courtier, without servility;
he was never reckoned among the Emperor's flatterers
before his fall or among his slanderers after. Napoleon
learned, on becoming First Consul, that Marshal de Ségur
was living at Versailles, in poor circumstances. He
desired Count de Ségur to bring his father to the
Tuileries. On his approach, the First Consul went to
meet him, and the consular guard forming the line
beat to arms. This token of honour, which had long
been suppressed, visibly affected the old General, to
whom at the same time Napoleon announced that his
pension of 6000 francs was restored, and that he might
draw six months' pay immediately.

In the early days of his astonishing fortune, Napoleon did not imitate the conduct of those up-starts who above all things dread witnesses to their first estate. He welcomed those who had known him in the past, rendered them services, and treated them with his former familiarity. The day he was appointed First Consul he despatched a courier to Saint Denis, bearing a letter to M. Rulhière, who had been a sub-lieutenant in the regiment of La Fère at the same time with himself, announcing that he had chosen him to be his secretary. He afterwards nominated him Secretary-General to the commission of government which he had just set up at Piedmont; and he finally gave him the prefecture of Aix-la-Chapelle. Rulhière did not live to take possession of this post: he had been attacked at Piedmont with a malady which all the art of medicine there could not define, and he died of it in Paris, whither he had gone for further advice.

As Napoleon grew older and stouter, his face became more rounded and his skin clearer, his eyes acquired lustre, and his countenance nobility, with a great deal of expression.

For three months after his marriage, the Emperor remained with the Empress night and day; even the most urgent affairs could not induce him to leave her for more than a few minutes. He, who had a passion for work, who would occupy himself with his Ministers for eight or ten consecutive hours without being fatigued, he who tired out secretary after secretary, now summoned councils at which he did not appear until two hours after they were assembled; he gave very few private audiences, and it was necessary to remind him several times of those which he could not possibly avoid granting. Such an alteration surprised every one; the Ministers were loud in their complaints; the old courtiers merely looked on, and said that such devotion was too extreme to last. The Empress was the only person who never doubted the permanence of a sentiment which she shared, and which made her happy.

Napoleon, it was said, had not always been thus amiable in private life. He was quick, choleric, irritable, and subject to a nervous affection (familiarly known as "the fidgets") which has given rise to scores of stories, one more ridiculous than another. It was even said that he was epileptic, subject to frequent attacks of the malady, and was occasionally unconscious for three or four hours at a time.

Nothing can be more absurd than these reports. I spoke of them to one of his personal attendants, who assured me that he had never seen anything to justify the popular belief, during six years which he had passed in Napoleon's service, and I can assert, on my own part, and during four years of my close attendance on the Empress, that I never perceived in the Emperor any symptom of such a complaint.

He was merry and familiar in private life; fond

of pulling ears and pinching cheeks, as Marshal Duroc, Berthier, Savary, and several of his aides-de-camp had reason to know. I have seen him, when present at the Empress's toilet, tease and plague her, pinching her neck and cheek. If he was vexed he took her in his arms, kissed her, called her *grosse bête*, and peace was made. Whenever the Emperor wished to play any of his tricks with Madame de Montebello, she repulsed him with ill-humour, and he left off immediately.

He was amiable and kind to all who were about him. Among a thousand instances of this, I will relate one. Every one knows that he was very fond of hunting. Berthier, who was then Grand Huntsman, liked the sport very well also, but he preferred pursuing it upon his own lands at Gros-Bois, to hunting with the Emperor. One day, after the season had begun, Berthier came to the "lever" of the Emperor, who asked him :

"What sort of weather is it ? "

"Bad weather, Sire."

"Will there be good hunting ?"

"No, Sire, there will be no scent."

"It must be put off, then."

The order was given, and at eleven o'clock the Emperor came to breakfast with the Empress. The sun was shining brightly; it was in the month of February. They agreed to go out walking, and to take Berthier. He was inquired for, and the Emperor was informed that he had gone off to hunt at Gros-

Bois. He laughed heartily at the trick which Berthier had played him, and vowed that he would never again take his word for the weather.

The Emperor would be master in important affairs, but he bore with contradiction, and even liked it. When he was in Marie-Louise's apartment he would tease the "first ladies" about all sorts of things. They would often hold their own against him, and he would go on with the discussion, and laugh heartily when our young people, who were very frank and artless, said things which pleased him by their bold simplicity.

One day he came into one of the salons, and there he found Mademoiselle M—— sitting with her back to the door. He made a sign to the ladies opposite to him to keep silence, and coming gently behind her, he popped his hands over her eyes. The only person she knew who could venture on such a familiarity with her was M. Bourdier, a respectable old gentleman, and First Physician to the Empress; so she never doubted that the intruder was he.

"Have done, M. Bourdier," she cried; "do you think I don't recognize your big ugly hands?" (The Emperor's hands were beautiful.)

"Big ugly hands," repeated the Emperor, restoring the use of her sight to her; "you are hard to please!"

The poor girl was so confused that she ran out of the room.

Another time, he was in the Empress's room while she was being dressed, and he inadvertently trod on the foot of the lady who presided at her Majesty's toilet. He immediately uttered a loud cry as though he had hurt himself.

"What is the matter with you?" asked the Empress.

"Nothing," said he, with a burst of laughter; "I trod on Madame D——'s foot, and I cried out, to prevent her from doing so; you see I have succeeded."

In the autumn which followed the Emperor's marriage, the Court passed some time at Fontainebleau. It was cold and damp in that vast palace. There were fires everywhere, except in the Empress's apartment; but she, being accustomed to stoves, objected to our fires, saying that they incommoded her. One day, the Emperor came to stay awhile with her, and on leaving the room he complained of the cold, and told the lady in attendance to have a fire lighted. When the Emperor was gone, the Empress forbid this to be done. The lady in attendance was Mademoiselle Rabusson, a young person who had just come from Écouen, and was very frank and natural. The Emperor returned two hours afterwards, and asked why his orders had not been executed.

"Sire," said the lady, "the Empress does not wish for a fire; she is in her own house (*chez elle*) and I am bound to obey her."

The Emperor laughed heartily at this answer. Going back to his own room, he found Duroc there, and said to him: "Do you know what I have just been told at the Empress's ? (*chez l'Imperatrice*) that the place is none of mine, and they won't let me have a fire there." This anecdote amused us all in the palace a good deal.

One day, when Napoleon was at breakfast with Marie-Louise, he perceived that he had forgotten his handkerchief. One was immediately brought him; he unfolded it, and observing that it was embroidered, and trimmed with lace, he inquired how much a handkerchief like that might cost.

"Well, from eighty to a hundred francs," answered Madame D——, to whom the question was addressed.

"If I were first lady," said he, "I would steal one every day."

"It is very lucky, Sire, that we have more honesty than your Majesty."

"That is well said," observed the Empress; "you have only got what you deserve."

The Emperor was much amused. He was very fond of children, and would often have the little sons of his brother Louis and Queen Hortense to breakfast with him and Marie-Louise. He liked to tease them. One day when the two little Princes were at breakfast, Louis,* aged three years and a half, was eating a boiled egg. Napoleon made him turn his head to look at a toy, and took away the egg. When the child missed it he took up his knife, and said to the Emperor :

"Give me back my egg, or I will kill you."

---

* Afterwards Napoleon III.—Translator's note.

"What, you rascal, would you kill your uncle?"

"I must have my egg, or I will kill you."

The Emperor gave it back to him, saying, "You will be a fine fellow."

Princess Elisa's daughter, a very proud child, of five, could not endure the jokes which the Emperor occasionally made at her expense, and said, after one of them, to her governess, who was present, "Let us return to Florence; I am not understood here."

Several instances of kindness and beneficence on the part of Napoleon are too well known for me to repeat them here; the following, I believe, has never been quoted. While hunting in the forest of Compiégne, he had dismounted, and was walking, accompanied only by the Duke of Vicenza, when he met two wood cutters who, being fatigued with their toil, were resting for a moment on the trunk of a tree. They had served with the French troops in the Egyptian expedition. One of the men recognized the Emperor and rose at once. M. de Caulaincourt wished to make the other stand up also.

"No, no," said Napoleon; "don't you see they are tired?"

He made the man who had risen sit down again, seated himself on the same tree trunk, talked to them about the expedition to Egypt, and their own affairs, and having learned that one of them had not obtained a retiring pension, he granted him one, and gave them ten Napoleons each on leaving them.

CHAPTER IV.

THE Emperor was not jealous, and yet he had surrounded his young wife with endless restrictions which resembled the precautions of jealousy. They had, however, their origin in less ungenerous ideas. He knew well the loose morals of his Court, and he wanted to organize a mode of life for the Empress which should render her inaccessible to the very lightest suspicion. The Lady-in-Waiting, the Lady of the Bedchamber, and the Lady Ushers, or Dames d'Annonces, exclusively possessed the right of entering her presence at all times. The Emperor, in organizing the household of the Empress, had very lofty views, as he had in everything else, but he was hindered in the carrying out of them by the petty passions of those around him.

In the time of the Empress Josephine, there were three Lady Ushers whose sole business was to keep the door of the private apartments. The Empress admitted several persons to intimacy with her; jealousies arose between the Ladies of the Palace and the Lady Ushers, and gave rise to disputes which worried and wearied Napoleon. This state of things induced the Emperor, who knew the sedentary life led by the ladies who devoted themselves to the education of the daughters of the members of the Legion of Honour in the imperial house of Écouen, to instruct the Queen of Naples to write to Madame Campan, the superintendent, requesting her to select four to be attached to the household of the Empress. He desired that the preference should be given to the daughters and widows of generals, and announced that for the future those places were to belong to the pupils of the imperial house at Écouen, and would be the reward of their good conduct. He kept his word; some months after, having raised the number of ladies to six, two of the pupils, Mesdemoiselles Materol and Rabusson, daughters and sisters of superior officers, were named. These six ladies, who at first bore the title of " Dames d'Annonces," because they had to announce the persons who presented themselves, but who were afterwards called " Premières Dames de l'Impératrice," because they were in reality charged with the whole of the personal service, had under their orders six waiting-women, but the latter did not come into the presence of the Empress except when they were summoned by a bell, while the former, four of whom were in waiting always, passed the entire day with her. They entered the Empress's room before she rose, and they never left her until she was in bed. Then all the doors by which access to her room was gained were shut, except one which led into an adjoining room; in this the ladies who had the principal "service" slept. The Emperor himself could enter his wife's room at night, only by passing through this one. No man, with the exception of the physicians or "Officers of Health," as they were called, and Messieurs de Maineval and Ballouhai—the former her "secretary of commands," the second her "steward of expenditure," was admitted into the private apartments of the Empress without an order from the Emperor. Even ladies, the Lady-in-Waiting, and the Lady of the Bedchamber only excepted, were not received until they had obtained an audience order from Marie-Louise. The Ladies of the Household were charged with the enforcement of these regulations, and responsible for their fulfilment. One of them was present at the lessons which the Empress received in music, drawing, and embroidery. They wrote to her dictation or by her order, and fulfilled the duties of readers. This was indisputably a wearisome life; but they had been accustomed to retirement at Écouen; the kindness of their imperial mistress mitigated its irksomeness, and they served her for love rather than from mere duty.

Their constant presence in the private rooms where the Emperor frequently came because the Empress passed a portion of her days there, excited the jealousy and envy of several Ladies of the Palace. As it was impossible to attack their conduct, which was perfectly correct, an attempt was made to humiliate them. It was at the solicitation of these ladies that Napoleon changed the title of " Dames d'Annonces " to that of " Premières femmes de chambre," a title which had no connection with the duties of the objects of their jealousy. The ladies of Écouen had nothing to do with the toilet of the Empress. One day, the Emperor, being at breakfast with the Empress, said to Madame D——, who was in attendance : " You ought to be glad, for I have given orders that captains of my guard are to be chosen as husbands for these young persons of yours."

" Sire, the captains of your guard will not marry waiting women " (*femmes de chambre*).

"And why not ? They will be presented after their marriage ; besides, was not Madame la Baronne de Misery *femme de chambre* to Marie-Antoinette ? "

" Since then, Sire, a revolution in ideas has taken place ; that which used to be held in honour is so held no longer. When your Majesty asked for ladies from Écouen to form part of the Empress's household, we had a right to believe that in quitting an honourable and respected position, we were not about to fall lower. But, Sire, ought I, the widow of a general,*

---

* General Durand commanded Fort Vauban in 1793 ; he was bombarded and obliged to surrender to the Austrians, after a most

and having a son, to make him blush for the position of his mother? If your Majesty persists in the intention of giving us this title, notwithstanding my profound grief at leaving the Empress, I shall beg of you to send me back to Écouen."

The Emperor laughed at my vehemence, and talked of something else. When he was gone, Marie-Louise, who was always kindness itself to me, asked me how I had dared to assert myself against the Emperor, and said she had been afraid that he might send me back to Écouen."

"Madame," I replied, "the Emperor is just, and he must have understood my susceptibility on the point."

A few days afterwards we were all six named " Lectrices " (Readers).

When the Court travelled, one of the First Ladies always slept in a room adjoining that of the Empress, and through which it was necessary to pass in order to reach her Majesty's.

I will cite two examples of the rigid observance of his rules exacted by the Emperor.

Biennais, the goldsmith, had had a coffer made for the Empress for the purpose of holding papers, with several secret contrivances in it; these were to be known to her alone, and it was indispensable that he

honourable defence. He was taken to Hungary. Being exchanged after the death of Robespierre, he retired into domestic life, and would not serve again. He died in 1807.

should show and explain them to her. Marie-Louise
spoke of the matter to her husband, who gave her
permission to receive Biennais, and the latter was
summoned to Saint-Cloud. He arrived, and was
shown into the music-room, where he remained at one
end with her Majesty, Madame D—— being in the
same room, but sufficiently far off not to hear the
explanation. Just as it was concluded, the Emperor
came in, and, seeing Biennais, he asked : "Who is that
man ?" The Empress hastened to name him, and to
explain why he had come, and that the Emperor himself had given permission for him to be admitted to
her presence. Napoleon distinctly denied the latter
assertion, declared that the lady on duty was in the
wrong, and addressed a severe reprimand to her which
the Empress had a great deal of trouble to check,
although she said to him :

"But, *mon ami*, it is I who gave orders that
Biennais should be sent for."

The Emperor laughed, and said it was no affair of
hers; that the lady on duty was responsible for those
who entered there ; that she only was to blame, and
he hoped the thing would not happen again.

The following is the second example. Marie-
Louise's music-master, M. Päer, had been her mother's
teacher also. One day, while he was giving her a
lesson, the lady on duty—again it was Madame D——
—had an order to transmit ; so she opened a door, and
standing, with half her body outside of it, gave the

order. At this moment Napoleon entered the room, and not seeing her at once, thought she was not there. After the music-master was gone, Napoleon asked where she had been when he came in. She told him that she had been in the room, but he would not believe her, and preached her a long sermon, in which he said he would not endure that any man, no matter of what rank, could boast of having been two seconds alone with the Empress. He added with vivacity:

"Madame, I honour and I respect the Empress; but the sovereign of a great Empire must be placed out of the reach of a suspicion."

After these two examples, it is easy to judge how much credit ought to be given to the anecdote which was so widely spread about, that Leroy, the Empress's tailor, had been excluded from the palace for having said to the Empress, while he was trying a dress on her, that she had beautiful shoulders. I know M. Leroy well enough to be quite sure that if he had been admitted to the Empress's private room he would not have said anything of the kind, for he has too much tact, and is too well versed in Court manners to commit such an impropriety; but, as a matter of fact, he never had the opportunity. Although the dresses ordered for Marie-Louise were made at his establishment, on a model which had been given to him, neither he nor anybody in his employment ever tried them on the Empress; it was her maids who showed him the alterations which he was to make. The same rule was observed with regard to the other milliners and dressmakers, male and female, the corset-maker, shoemaker, glover, etc. No purveyor of any kind of wares whatever either saw or spoke to the Empress in private.

CHAPTER V.

MADAME DE MONTEBELLO, Lady-in-Waiting, and
Madame de Luçay, Lady of the Bedchamber, passed
an hour or two every morning with the Empress. One
might be tempted to believe that a fatality attaches
to those two posts, for at no time in the history of the
Court of France have the ladies who occupied them
been able to live together in peace. The Memoirs of
Mesdames de Motteville and Campan prove the truth
of this observation; here is a fresh example.

Madame de Montebello and Madame de Luçay
never liked each other from the time they were
attached to the service of the Empress, and it appears
that the former had done very ill turns to the latter.

An estrangement ensued, which was the more
remarkable because it originated with Madame de
Montebello, and the more surprising because Madame
de Luçay is amiable, well bred, perfect in her conduct

and demeanour, incapable of harming even an enemy
(if she could have one), with no courage to defend herself, and only able to summon any when it is a case of
defending the absent; and she possesses all the habits
and manners of Court life, having lived at Court several
years.   Her husband had been one of the first to
attach himself to the fortunes of Napoleon; he was
then owner of the Château de Valençay, and was
appointed Prefect of Indre; he afterwards became
Prefect of the Palace, and Madame de Luçay was made
Lady of the Palace to Josephine.   The Emperor, who
had every reason to be pleased with her, placed her in
the service of his young wife as Lady of the Bedchamber.

Madame de Montebello belonged to the bourgeois
class.   Her mother, who was an estimable woman, had
presided over her education; but, not having lived in
high society, she could not impart to her daughter
either the ideas or the sentiments which she would
have needed, to enable her adequately to fill so
important a post.

She appeared at Court as the wife of General
Lannes; she had a virginal face and an air of great
sweetness; she pleased everybody, although in reality
there was a great deal of coldness and hardness in her
nature.   She was not often at Court at first, because her husband required her to follow him in his
expeditions.   General Lannes, who was born in the
plebeian class, had merited and won the friendship

and favour of Napoleon by deeds of distinguished
valour, and when a new nobility was created the title
of duke was conferred upon him.   But Lannes was not
content with this, and said openly that he deserved
the title of prince better than any of those who had
obtained it.   His frankness was extreme, and he was
almost the only man who never disguised his real
thoughts from the Emperor.   He supremely detested
the old nobility, especially the *emigrés*, and he had
done all in his power to dissuade Napoleon from
recalling them to France, and above all from attaching
them to his person.   He had, indeed, had some sharp
quarrels on this point with the Empress Josephine, who
was on their side.   He did not attempt to conceal this
aversion: the *emigrés*, who were informed of it,
heartily reciprocated his sentiments.

One day there happened to be several of the recalled nobles in one of the salons of the Tuileries
through which Lannes had to pass, on his way to the
Emperor's cabinet, and they affected to place themselves
before him so as to bar his way.   The General instantly
drew his sword, and swore he would crop the ears of
anybody who should hinder him from passing.   He
found no obstacle ; every one there hastened to get out
of his way, for he was a man of his word.

On another occasion, when he had been vainly
urging Napoleon anew on the subject of the *emigrés*,
and entreating him to refuse to admit any one of them
near him, he at last lost control of himself, and, using

the old familiar *tutoiement* as he had been accustomed
to use it a few years before, he said :

"Thou wilt never do anything except out of thine
own head! but thou wilt repent of this. They are
traitors; thou shalt load them with benefits, and if
they get the opportunity they will assassinate thee."

This outbreak was punished by the General's temporary exile, and as he imputed that also to the
emigrés, it did not diminish his enmity against
them. But it was Murat for whom he most openly
paraded his contempt. Murat, who belonged to the
lower order of the people, was destined, like Masaniello,
to exercise the supreme authority at Naples, and also,
like him, to end his days in a no less tragic manner,
with, however, this difference, that he retained to the
last the strength of mind and courage which had been
characteristic of him all his life.

He was renowned in the army for his personal
courage, although his companions in arms did not
consider that he possessed the chief qualities which
constitute a great general.

Josephine said of Murat (whom she liked no better
than she liked his wife), "He smells of powder half
a league off, and would put his Creator to the
sword." Murat's marriage with the Emperor's sister
was one of the principal causes of his elevation. Even
at that period the First Consul would not have allowed
his brother-in-law to continue to be merely one among
the generals of the Republic. He always placed him

at the head of his advanced guard, and Murat's dashing gallantry had a success that was never equivocal.

Murat loved show and expense, and more than once he had recourse to the generosity of his brother-in-law, who paid his debts for him; not, however, without reprimanding him severely for his prodigality, and the luxury in which he indulged even in the field. When he was made prince, he visited the Department of the Lot, where he was born, and his family still resided. He assembled all its members, rich and poor, at a great dinner, and inquired into the circumstances of each. Some of his relations were very poor, but the new prince was not ashamed of any of them. Every one belonging to him was enabled to live comfortably by his beneficent aid.

But, to return to Marshal Lannes. It is not surprising that he inspired his wife with feelings similar to his own, and she afterwards gave more than one proof of them. Her private circle was composed of her family, and the only stranger whom she received was Dr. Corvisart, first physician to the Emperor at Guichénene. Her father was an intimate friend of the doctor, to whom he was bound by a community of tastes and habits, and this society was not what might have been desired for a young woman destined to a high position near the throne.

At the period of which I write the Duchess was just thirty years old; in full dress she was one of the best-looking women belonging to the Court. Her expression was calm and gentle; she had a cold manner which she could render gracious when she chose. As she loved only her children and her kinsfolk, she had always enjoyed a spotless reputation, and to this she owed the place of Lady-in-Waiting (or *Dame d'honneur*), which the Emperor said he had given her because she was truly "a lady of honour." If, however, her behaviour made her suitable for the post, her disposition did not. Madame de Montebello, loving her home and her ease, detesting every kind of restraint, naturally indolent and inactive, disliking the duties which took her so completely out of her own ways, never took any pleasure in her position. She dreaded having to make requests, to solicit anything, and yet she was obliged to do so for many persons, whose number increased as she grew in favour, and she made enemies of those whom she forgot or neglected. She had not the art of refusing gracefully: her negative answers were abrupt and harsh, and whether she was obtaining a favour or employed to announce a granted grace, it was done in the same way, as a matter in which she took no personal interest whatsoever.

This conduct alienated a number of persons whom she might have attached to her by one gracious word. She was reproached with being lofty and exacting with her equals, proud and disdainful with her inferiors. She thought it beneath her to conceal her opinion of those who were the subject of remark, and she expressed it openly and without reserve. This frankness, so novel at Court, won the confidence of the Empress, but it also made enemies for her who sought their revenge in spreading a most unfounded calumny concerning her. It was reported that she was with child by Napoleon. Now, Madame Lannes never even liked the Emperor; I believe, indeed, that she had a positive dislike to him.

It is asserted that the reason of her dislike was to be found in her ambition. She had deeply resented her husband's not having been made prince, regarding this as an injustice ; perhaps she was right. The death of the Marshal increased her bitterness against Napoleon, but her anger reached its culminating point when she had a request made to the Emperor, through the Empress, that the Senatorship of Douay, vacant by the death of Jacqueminot, might be given to her father, and it was refused in the most ungracious way. The story against her was trumped up in the hope of discrediting her with the Empress, but its falsehood was so evident that only those who would swallow anything, gave credence to it. The Duchess was apprised that such a rumour was in circulation, and did not allow a day to pass without presenting herself at the Tuileries. It is untrue that she was ever absent ; the duties of her post were fulfilled at that period with unfailing exactness.

This occurrence ought to have induced her to take some pains to conciliate certain ladies of the Palace who detested her, constantly complained of her, and said that she could never be half an hour in the *salon de service* without saying something unpleasant to them. She was not much better liked at home; and this was a remarkable fact, for she was endowed with qualities calculated to please and to win regard.

It is said that, although she was very rich, Corvisart, who was her friend, had persuaded Marie-Louise that Madame Lannes had only 6000 francs a year, out of the immense fortune of her husband, and that she, on her side, rendered a similar service to the doctor by representing to the Empress that he was in embarrassed circumstances. The result of this concerted manœuvre was that the Duchess and the doctor received handsome donations and presents.

When, in 1813, Napoleon granted a pension of 50,000 francs to Madame de Montesquiou as a recompense for the care she had bestowed upon his son, Madame de Montebello was so angry and jealous that she gave the Empress no rest until she had obtained a like favour for her from the Emperor, although she had done nothing to merit it, and ought to have been ashamed to solicit any such thing.

After a few months the Emperor resumed his former habits, worked more steadily, and was less assiduous in his attentions to his young wife.

Marie-Louise felt that she needed a friend, and the Duchess de Montebello listened with sympathy to the outpourings of her royal mistress's heart, bemoaned her, pitied her, consoled her, and insinuated herself so cleverly into her confidence and good graces that the Empress could not do without her. She loved the Duchess like a sister, and sought to prove this to her by the kindest attentions both to herself and her children. She was happy to find a present which could please the Duchess, and to offer it to her in a frank and graceful manner which was very charming; she liked those whom her friend liked, and disliked all who were displeasing to her. The ascendency of the Duchess was observed, and she was speedily accused by persons who considered that they had a right to complain.

Of the number were the Emperor's sisters, and Madame Mère spoke very sharply on the subject to the Empress, complaining of Madame de Montebello. The latter, being informed of this, and finding herself obliged to make a visit to Madame, said in the presence of three of the *femmes de chambre*, and a first lady, that she despised what Madame said, and that she wished she could write upon her card that her visit was for the mother of the Emperor, and not for " Madame Mère."

Those words " Madame Mère " remind me of an amusing anecdote which I shall relate here, although it be somewhat out of place, lest I should not find another opportunity : for it deserves to be preserved.

A certain prefect of a department (one of the most distant from the capital), having been summoned to

Paris, received an invitation to dine with Cambacères the day after his arrival. The palace of the minister adjoined that of the Emperor's mother, and the prefect, mistaking the door, entered the abode of Madame, instead of that of the Arch-Chancellor. It happened that it was one of her grand reception days, and the prefect, having given his name, was ushered into a salon where a large number of persons were assembled. He looked about everywhere for Cambacères, and not seeing him, took his place in the circle without addressing a word to anybody.

"Excuse me for taking a liberty," said a neighbour on one side of him, "but it seems to me that you have not made your bow to Madame."

"Madame whom?" said the stranger, who knew that Cambacères was not married.

"Madame Mère," answered his neighbour.

"But mother of whom?" (Mère de qui?)

"Mother of his Majesty the Emperor."

"Am I not in Cambacères' house?"

"You are in the Emperor's mother's house."

The poor prefect, overwhelmed with confusion, took his departure in all haste, and had not even sufficient presence of mind to offer an apology. Ever since he is known by the nickname of "M. le Prefect Mère de qui."

CHAPTER VI.

AN occasion on which the Duchess de Montebello
appeared in a very favourable light was the birth
of the son of Napoleon. It is well known that the
Empress suffered very severely in her confinement, and
for nine whole days Madame de Montebello remained
in her room, hardly ever leaving it for a moment. She
passed the nights upon a sofa; in short, she did
everything that could have been expected from either
her sense of duty or her feelings of affection.

In writing of the Empress's confinement, it is fitting
that I should give some details relating to the birth of
the child concerning whom the most absurd rumours
were then rife. According to some of these the
Empress had never been pregnant, and her delivery
was a comedy played for the purpose of enabling
Napoleon to adopt one of his natural children.
According to others, Marie-Louise had been delivered
of a still-born daughter, for whom another child had

been substituted. These reports, as ridiculous as they
were improbable, were without the very slightest
foundation, and the short narrative which follows may
be confidently accepted as certain and authentic.

It was seven o'clock in the evening when the
Empress felt the first pains of childbirth. M. Dubois,
the surgeon-accoucheur, was summoned, and he re-
mained with her thenceforth. The pains went on
during the whole night. With the Empress were
Madame de Montebello, Madame de Luçay, Madame
de Montesquiou (who had been appointed governess to
the child about to be born), two first ladies, Mesdames
Durand and Ballant, and Madame Blaise, the nurse.
The Emperor, his mother, his sisters, and MM
Corvisart and Bourdier, were in an adjoining room.
They frequently entered the room to learn how the
Empress was, but observed the most profound silence.
The pains, which had not been strong during the night
subsided altogether at five o'clock in the morning.
M. Dubois, seeing no symptom that indicated a speedy
deliverance, informed the Emperor, and he, having sent
everybody to bed, went to his bathroom. There
remained in the Empress's room only M. Dubois and
the ladies whom I have named. The other women
attached to her service were resting in the adjoining
dressing-room.

The Empress, worn out with fatigue, slept for about
an hour; she was then awakened by violent pains,
which went on increasing in severity without, how-

ever, producing the natural crisis, and M. Dubois was
only too sadly certain that the accouchement would be
difficult and protracted.   He went to the Emperor, who
was then in the bath, and begged him to come to the
Empress, to encourage her by his presence to bear her
sufferings with courage.   M. Dubois did not conceal
from him that he feared it would be impossible to save
both mother and child.   "Think only of the mother!"
cried Napoleon, "and do all you can for her."   He
would hardly let himself be dried; and went to the
Empress's room, having given orders that all those
who ought to be present should be apprised.   He embraced his wife tenderly, and exhorted her to courage
and patience.   M. Bourdier, physician, and M. Yvan,
surgeon, arrived at this moment, and they held Marie-
Louise.   The child was born feet foremost; M. Dubois
was obliged to resort to instruments in order to free
the head.   The delivery lasted for twenty-six minutes,
and was very painful.   The Emperor could not remain
present for more than five minutes.   He relinquished
the hand of the Empress, which he had been holding
between his own, and withdrew to the dressing-room.
He was as pale as death, and seemed to be beside himself.   Almost every minute he sent one of the women
to bring him news of his wife.   At length the child
came into the world, and so soon as the Emperor was
told, he flew to his wife and folded her in his
arms.

The infant remained for seven minutes without

E

any sign of life. Napoleon cast his eyes upon it for
an instant, thought it was dead, did not utter a single
word, but occupied himself solely with the Empress.
A few drops of brandy were put into the child's
mouth, its whole body was slapped with the flat of
the hand, and it was wrapped in hot cloths. At
length it uttered a cry, and the Emperor turned to
embrace the son, whose birth was the crowning point
of his happiness, and the last gift of that fortune
which was so soon to forsake him.

This scene took place in the presence of twenty-
two persons, whom it will be well to name, in order
to establish the authenticity of the details which I
have just given. The witnesses were the Emperor.
Cambacérès, who, as Arch-chancellor of the Empire,
had to attest the sex and the birth of the infant; the
Prince de Neufchatel, who, although he had no official
business there, attended the Emperor, from zeal and
attachment; MM. Dubois, Corvisart, Bourdier, and
Yvan; Mesdames de Montebello, de Luçay, and de
Montesquiou; the six first ladies, Mesdames Ballant,
Deschamps, Durand, Hureau, Rabusson, and Gérard;
five waiting-women, Mesdemoiselles Honoré, Edouard,
Barbier, Aubert, and Geoffroy; Madame Blaise (the
nurse), and two wardrobe-maids. This sufficiently
demonstrates the absurdity of the fable of a suppo-
sititious child. The thing could not have been done
in the presence of so many witnesses, and it should
also be borne in mind that adjoining the bedroom on

one side was the dressing-room, crowded with all the subordinate persons employed in the service of Marie-Louise, and on the other were several salons occupied by a number of persons belonging to the Court, who were all impatiently awaiting news of the important event that was impending.

All the inhabitants of Paris knew that the Empress had been seized with the pains of labour, and from six o'clock in the morning the garden of the Tuileries was filled with an immense crowd of people of all ages and conditions. It had been made known that twenty-one guns would announce the birth of a princess; but that one hundred and one would be fired to celebrate that of an heir to the throne. No sooner was the first gun fired than profound silence fell upon the multitude, just before so restless and noisy. This silence was broken only by those who counted the reports of the guns, saying, in a low voice, one, two, three, etc. But, at the twenty-second, the enthusiasm of all broke out simultaneously, cries of joy, hats tossed in the air, and shouts from the garden of the Tuileries contributed as much as did the roar of the guns to carry the great news to the other quarters of Paris. Napoleon, hidden behind the curtain of a window of the Empress's room, enjoyed the spectacle of the general gladness, and was deeply affected by it. Tears rolled down his cheeks without his feeling them flow, and it was in this state that he came to embrace his son anew.

Without giving a complete list of the poems, epistles, odes, strophes, couplets, etc., etc., written in all the living languages (English excepted) which were composed on the occasion of the birth of the King of Rome, I will only say that the number of compositions of this kind sent to the Emperor and Empress amounted to over two thousand in less than a week. The Emperor accepted them all (without reading them, it is true), and with them the requests for favours of all kinds which the authors had, with wise foresight, added to their effusions. How, indeed, could Napoleon, who was naturally generous, refuse tokens of his goodwill to those who expatiated upon the bounty of Providence towards himself? It was impossible, and any other individual in his place would have done as much. I have it on good authority that a sum of one hundred thousand francs, charged upon his privy purse, was divided by M. Dequevanvilliers, Accountant-Secretary of the Chamber, among the authors of the effusions sent to the Tuileries.

A curious fact, to whose authenticity I can pledge myself, is, that when Napoleon, having returned from the island of Elba, left Paris to take the command of the army assembled on the frontiers of Flanders, one of these poets of the moment, assisted by two others, composed a dramatic piece destined for the Théâtre des Variétés, which could be made, by a few trifling alterations, to do equally well for the celebration of the triumph of Napoleon, or the return of Louis XVIII.

Immediately after its birth the imperial infant was confided to a nurse of healthy and robust constitution, taken from the class of "the people." She could not go out of the palace, or be visited by any man ; the most stringent precautions were taken in that respect. For health's sake she was regularly taken out in a carriage, but she was always accompanied by several women.

I have already said that the Countess de Montesquiou, whose husband was Grand Chamberlain, had been appointed governess to the young Napoleon. It would have been difficult to make a better choice. This lady, who came of an illustrious family, had received an excellent education ; to the "ton" of the great world she united piety too sincere and enlightened ever to degenerate into bigotry. Her conduct had always been such as calumny itself dared not attack. She was accused of some haughtiness, but this was tempered by politeness, and a gracious obligingness. She took the most tender and assiduous care of the young Prince, and nothing could be more noble and generous than the self-devotion which afterwards led her to leave her country, her friends, and her family, to ally herself with the fate of a child, all whose hopes had just been laid low. And yet the only reward she reaped was bitter grief and unjust persecution.

CHAPTER VII.

THE THREE ARM-CHAIRS—THE EMPRESS'S MEDICINE—THE THREE PARTIES
—JOURNEY TO FONTAINEBLEAU—BULL OF EXCOMMUNICATION SENT
BY THE POPE—THE ABBÉ D'ASTROS—THE DUKE OF ROVIGO—THE
DIRECTOR-GENERAL OF THE LIBRARY—COUNT BIGOT DE PRÉAMENEU,
MINISTER OF PUBLIC WORSHIP—VISIT TO THE POPE.

For six weeks after the birth of her child, Marie-
Louise received only the Lady-in-Waiting, the Lady of
the Bedchamber, and the Princesses of the Imperial
family. When Madame Mère or one of the sisters of
Napoleon came to see her, arm-chairs were placed for
them near her bed. On the day appointed for Marie-
Louise to receive, for the first time, all the persons
presented at Court, the Emperor remarked that three
arm-chairs, for Madame Mère and the Queens of Spain
and Holland respectively, had been placed near the
state couch prepared for the Empress. He found fault
with this arrangement; said that his mother, not being
a queen, ought not to have an arm-chair, and therefore
no one should have it. He ordered the arm-chairs to be
removed, and three very elegant tabourets put in their
places. Madame Mère arrived presently, with the two

queens, and when they found that they were not to
have arm-chairs they withdrew at once with an
offended air, and would not remain to take part in
the reception of the ladies who were expected. This
incident increased the coolness which already existed
in the private relations of the family, and a number of
small annoyances resulted from it, the brunt of which
the Empress had to bear, although she was entirely
blameless in the matter of their origin.

One day when Marie-Louise was to take medicine,
she insisted on its being given to her before her doctor
arrived. After she had swallowed the dose she had a
sharp attack of cholic, and this gave rise to some
uneasiness. The Emperor was informed, and came
hurriedly to her room. She was over the attack,
but he lectured the Duchess de Montebello at great
length on the imprudence she had committed in allow-
ing the Empress to take a medicine without being
prepared for its effect, and repeated several times,
" Etiquette requires that it shall be the doctor who
presents the medicine." The Duchess made no answer,
but when the Emperor was gone she said, "I am glad
M. l'Etiquette has done : I never liked long sermons."

At this period Napoleon visited the coasts of
France. The Empress had as yet hardly recovered
from her confinement, and the Emperor wished her to
remain in Paris, but she urged him so strongly to
allow her to accompany him that he could not refuse.
She became considerably thinner during this journey,

no doubt in consequence of the fatigue which she endured; and she never recovered her former plumpness.

The French Court was then divided into three parties, the old nobility, the new nobility, and the military. Madame de Montesquiou and her husband were at the head of the first. All the influence they had was used to obtain favours, pensions, and places for the nobles, whether *emigrés* or not; they represented to the Emperor that by such means they would be more securely attached to his person, and brought to regard his government with affection. They said these things because they genuinely and sincerely thought them; and because, believing the destiny of France to be for ever fixed, they desired to attach to the sovereign those persons who ought in their opinion to be the strongest supporters of the Empire. Napoleon fully recognized their zeal and devotion; he was a witness of the indefatigable care bestowed upon his son by Madame de Montesquiou, and he seldom refused her anything which she asked.

After what I have said of Madame de Montebello, it will at once be surmised that she was the soul of the second party. It was not numerous at Court, being composed in great measure of second-rate schemers, but it was sustained by the consideration in which Marie-Louise held her favourite.

The third party was headed by General Duroc, and was composed, to speak generally, of all who were connected with military matters. This party saw no

honour or glory outside the profession of arms, and
had a sovereign contempt for every other. While
the first and second parties carried on open warfare,
endeavouring to injure and destroy each other by
every possible means, the third played the part of
observer, unmasked their schemes, and profited by
their faults and blunders. The Emperor secretly
favoured this third party; but none the less did he
pursue his usual system of neutralizing all opinions by
endeavouring to balance their forces. Each party
served as a spy upon the two others, and by this
means he was informed of all that it was his interest
to know.

The Duchess de Montebello and the Countess de
Montesquiou being at the head of two parties which
were not only different but antagonistic, it may readily
be supposed that no very intimate relations subsisted
between them. The Countess, always prudent and reserved, did not proclaim her dislike to the Duchess.
and did not seek to do her any ill. She was satisfied
with never speaking of her, and conducting the inevitable intercourse imposed by their respective posts
with extreme coldness. But this was not the case
with Madame de Montebello. She went as seldom as
possible to see the little Prince, in order that she might
not be obliged to see his governess at the same time.
She endeavoured to persuade the Empress that the
care which Madame de Montesquiou took of her son,
the affection for him that she displayed, had no motive

except ambition and self-interest, an accusation amply disproved by later events. Madame de Montesquiou, being informed of these continual efforts to injure her, complained of them once or twice to the Empress, and endeavoured to open her eyes with respect to her favourite; but the first impression had been made, and we all know the strength of a first impression, especially when it is received in youth, and produced by a person to whom all one's confidence is given.

Marie-Louise did not then do Madame de Montesquiou the justice that was due to her, as she had occasion to recognize in later days.

At this period the Emperor went to Fontainebleau for ten days. He did not like the prolongation of his differences with the Pope. The long-continued quarrel between the Holy Father and Napoleon dated from 1805. When Pius VII. left France after the coronation, it was with secret annoyance at not having obtained the rewards that he considered due to him. Hardly had he set his foot on Italian soil before intrigues were organized, and pamphlets written, profiting by his discontent to overrule his mind and direct his intentions. Rome became the hotbed of all the political intrigues and plots against the tranquility of France.

His Holiness had refused to recognize the validity of the Emperor's divorce from Josephine, and consequently that of his marriage with Marie-Louise. An open rupture had taken place between them in consequence, and Pius VII., listening to nothing but the indiscreet zeal of some of his advisers, had launched the thunderbolts of the Vatican against Napoleon. The sentence of excommunication had been sent from Rome to Paris, to the Abbé d'Astros, Vicar Capitular of the Archbishopric (the See was vacant), who had it printed, and affixed it to the door of Notre Dame, in the presence of some of the Canons on whose discretion he could rely. Copies of the Papal Brief were very soon spread all over Paris, and thence throughout the provinces. It was asserted that the Director-General of Printing and Publication had been informed of this, but had taken no measures to check the proceeding, nor had he even informed the Emperor.

The Duke of Rovigo, Minister of Police, was one of the first to be informed of what had occurred, and as he had been for a long time on terms of rivalry with the Director, he took advantage of this opportunity to present a circumstantial report to Napoleon, in which that functionary was not flattered.

On perusing this document the Emperor fell into a transport of rage difficult to describe. He was expected that day at the Council of State, and he came in violently agitated. Every one present remarked the change in his face, but no one said a word, no one moved. Napoleon walked hurriedly about the Council Chamber, uttering incoherent and half-formed sentences: the only word that could be heard distinctly was "bigot," an epithet which he probably applied to the Abbé d'Astros.

Bigot de Préameneu, a Councillor of State, was present at the sitting. The word "bigot" had caught his ear several times, and he thought the Emperor was calling him.

"Sire," said he, rising.

"What do you want?" said Napoleon.

"Sire, I thought your Majesty spoke to me."

"Not at all—yes, though, yes—a moment. Bigot, I appoint you Minister of Public Worship" (Cultes). After such a fashion was this new ministry instituted.

The Director-General of Printing and Publication, who was also a Councillor of State, arrived at this moment, and was about to take his usual place.

"Stay," said the Emperor, "and answer me. Do you know what took place last Sunday at Notre Dame? Don't stammer; no jesuitical equivocation."

"Sire, I knew that——"

"Ah, you knew it! and you did not inform me of it. I was publicly reviled, and you kept silence! They dare to publish a Bull of Excommunication against me in the middle of my capital, and you let it pass like that!"

"Sire, I thought that in proceeding publicly against a man who believed he was doing his duty, I should only secure the interest that always attaches to a martyr for him. I thought oblivion was a duty which——"

"Your duty! Your duty! The first of all, sir, was to consult me. I am grieved in all this for the memory of your father—I don't suspect you of evil intentions—but— There, there, go and sit down."

And the matter rested there for the moment.

A few days afterwards, however, the Abbé d'Astros was obliged, according to custom, to wait upon the Emperor at the head of the Chapter of Notre Dame, in order to offer him the compliments of the new year. At the sight of him all that had passed at the Council of State recurred to Napoleon's mind, and revived his wrath; he strode towards the Abbé with a threatening gesture, and exclaimed—

"Hah! It is you, then, who want to light the fire of sedition in my realm! It is you who betray your sovereign to execute the orders of a foreign priest! I will have neither revolt, nor fanaticism, nor a martyr. I am a Christian, and more Christian than you all. I shall know how to maintain the right of my crown against those who resemble you. God has armed me with the sword—let not you and your like forget that."

The Abbé d'Astros attempted to reply, but an imperative gesture of the Emperor obliged him to desist and retire. The matter rested there. Nevertheless, it has been maintained by many people, and even recorded in writing, that the Abbé d'Astros fell a victim to his apostolic zeal, having been disgraced, thrown into prison, and persecuted. This again, is one of the malicious falsehoods which have been so widely disseminated.

It is a fact which will be more and more clearly demonstrated as time goes on, that Napoleon loved his religion, that he desired to make it prosper and to honour it, but at the same time to make use of it as a social means of repressing anarchy, consolidating his domination over Europe, and increasing the importance of France and the influence of the inhabitants of Paris; objects on which his thoughts were constantly intent.

During this period the Pope had been carried away from his States, taken to Savona, and brought from thence to Fontainebleau, where he occupied the apartment which had been assigned to him on the former occasion.* A household was formed for him, and his table was magnificently served; but he did not avail himself of this. He lived in the most retired rooms, and in the simplest and most frugal manner. His suite only sat down to the splendid repasts. Napoleon had been forming for a long time a secret design of renewing relations with Pius VII., and in order to carry it out more easily, he gave orders for a hunting-party at Gros-Bois, where he breakfasted. Then, quite unexpectedly, he directed the road to Fontainebleau to be taken. The confusion which this unforeseen journey occasioned was very amusing. Nobody had a man or a maid, a night cap or any dressing

---

* See Memoirs of Madame de Rémusat for details of the Pope's visit to France. the coronation of Napoleon and Josephine, and the celebration of the religious marriage between them.—Translator's note.

things; it was bitterly cold, water froze close up to the fire. Everybody passed a very bad night, but in the morning our baggage and servants arrived from Paris.

We remained nine days at Fontainebleau. The Emperor paid a visit to the Pope, and his Holiness came to see the Emperor. There were several conferences, and a reconciliation seemed probable. At the moment of our departure the Pope was ill, and kept his bed. We went to beg that he would bless some rings and rosaries for us; they were taken to him in his bed, and he was so good as to grant our request.

CHAPTER VIII.

NAPOLEON'S GALLANTRIES—MADAME WALEWSKA—THE CHÂTEAU DE
COMPIÈGNE—GRAZINI AND BODE—FOUCHÉ, MINISTER OF GENERAL
POLICE.

I HAVE already said that the Emperor had organized
his private police. He did not make any political
use of this branch of the service; it furnished him
with a source of amusement. He liked to be acquainted
with all the current scandals concerning the persons
of his Court, and he took a special pleasure in teasing
husbands about the adventures of their wives.

At this point I must refer to Napoleon's gallantries.
A great many false statements on the subject have
been circulated and printed, and he has been charged
with intriguing with women of whom he never even
thought. It is well known that he never had a *maîtresse en titre* ; it must not, however, be concluded from
this that he had not passing inclinations and fancies
which it was easy for him, in his position, to gratify.
But he was as careful to conceal his own gallantries
as he was ready to talk of those of other people, and

above all, he was totally free from the folly of boasting of favours which have not been obtained.

In his youth he had been much attached to Madame Walewska, a Polish lady (he made her acquaintance during the campaign of 1806–7), and she was one of the two women who retained his friendship and regard after the cessation of all other relations with them. Madame Walewska never ceased to give him proofs of sincere affection. On the occasion of his abdication, she went to Fontainebleau to take leave of him, and when she learned that Marie-Louise had not accompanied him to the Island of Elba, she went thither, taking her son, whose father Napoleon was, with the intention of remaining merely as a friend whose society might be agreeable to him. To this, however, Napoleon would not consent. He would not inflict upon his wife the mortification of knowing that a woman whom he had formerly loved, although before his marriage with her, was with him. Madame Walewska stayed at Elba for three days only.

There was a great deal of scandal, formerly, about the Emperor's adventures with two celebrated actresses, and in the first edition of this work I referred to the subject. I have, however, suppressed the mention of those ladies in the present edition, in consequence of the strictures of several newspapers. No doubt Napoleon was a very unfaithful husband to Josephine. It is a fact that in the Château de Compiègne a secret suite of rooms was constructed, opening from the

F

corridor on which the ladies' "lodging," as it was
called, was situated; and access to these rooms, which
did not appear to form a portion of the particular
allotment, was provided by a single small door, looking like that of a mere passage, which might be
completely overlooked. This suite, composed of several
charming rooms, faced the park, and commanded an
extensive and delightful view; it was furnished with
taste; luxury and elegance were combined in its
decorations. Lastly, although it was at a long distance from the Emperor's own apartment, a secret
staircase connected the two. I visited the rooms myself
after Napoleon's second marriage. They were no
longer used, and therefore no longer so carefully con-
cealed. No doubt he did avail himself of them, but not
to the extent that has been alleged. The gallantries
of the Emperor have been grossly exaggerated; by
some, in order to make him ridiculous; by others, for
the purpose of representing him as an immoral man;
while there are actually persons so corrupt as to think
it redounds to his glory and renown to depict him as a
great conqueror of women, most of whom were ready
to meet him half, and many three-fourths, of the way.

The following anecdote, which I have on good
authority, although the fact that gave rise to it
occurred in Josephine's time, illustrates what I have
just said. As it is known to a few persons only, I
think it well to introduce it in this chapter.

Napoleon, having been struck by the showy beauty

of Grazini, the singer, when he had passed through
Naples, made overtures to her, and sent her valuable
presents. He employed Berthier to conclude a treaty
with her on a very liberal basis, and to bring her to
Paris; in fact, she made the journey in Berthier's
own carriage. She was allowed twenty thousand
francs a month; and she made a splendid figure
at the theatres, and at concerts at the Tuileries.
But then, as I have already said, the Chief of the
State avoided all scandal, and did not wish to give
umbrage to Josephine, who was excessively jealous, so
that he paid only brief and furtive visits to the fair
singer. La Grazini (as she was called at the château)
was a proud and passionate woman, in whose imagin-
ation, as well as in her voice, there was something
masculine, and she could not brook such desultory and
careless attention; she therefore resorted to the in-
fallible antidote, and fell violently in love with the
celebrated violin-player, Rode, who reciprocated her
feelings. The lovers were too ardent to be careful,
and even braved the vigilance of Berthier himself.

One day the Emperor sent for Fouché, then Minister
of General Police, and told him he was astonished, that
with all his well-known skill, he (Fouché) did not
do his business better, and that things were going on
which he knew nothing about.

"Yes," replied the vexed minister, "things do go
on which I did know nothing about, but I know all
about them now! For instance, a short man, wearing

a blue cloak and a three-cornered hat, comes out of the château every second day, between eight and nine o'clock in the evening, by the side gate of the Marsan pavilion, over the kitchens, and gets into a hackney-coach, with a man taller than himself, but dressed in the same way,* and drives straight to Grazini's, 28, Rue Chantereine. The little man is yourself, and the sly cantatrice deceives you in favour of Rode, the fiddler, who lives at the Hotel de l'Empire, Rue du Mont Blanc."

At this, Napoleon turned his back on his minister, and began to walk up and down with his hands behind his back, whistling an Italian air. Fouché withdrew without another word.

Napoleon was but rarely unfaithful to Marie-Louise, and he took the greatest care to prevent the very few infidelities in which he indulged from coming to her knowledge; for he always treated her with the utmost consideration. He did, however, occasionally lament that she would not make herself agreeable to the ladies of the Court, and exert herself a little more to please. He had been accustomed to the unfailing grace, and the unvarying amiability of Josephine, and he certainly could not fail to remark a difference between his first wife and his second; but he forgot that the latter, born in the purple, accustomed from her infancy to homage and respect, and of a naturally shy and reserved disposition, knew nothing whatever

* Duroc, Grand Marshal.

of the mind of the French nation, and had no one about her who was in a position to advise, guide, and make her understand how essential it was, not only for her own, but for her son's sake, that she should win their regard. But, although the Empress had the defect of being cold and impassive in public, the blame ought not to be laid to her account. She was constantly told that one ought to be natural, and to appear just as one is; an excellent principle in private life, no doubt, but it does not work in the case of sovereigns, or indeed in that of the great, who require to do many kindnesses, and to be very condescending in order to make the lower classes like them.

CHAPTER IX.

MARIE-LOUISE AND JOSEPHINE COMPARED — GENEROSITY OF THE TWO EMPRESSES — INFANCY OF NAPOLEON'S SON — A PETITION ADDRESSED TO THE KING OF ROME—THE BRINGING-UP OF THE YOUNG PRINCE.

To gain the hearts of the French, one need only know how to smile and bow at the right time. It pleases them to consider their sovereign as the head, or father of that large family, and a little affability amply repays them for the respect and affection with which they regard him. Marie-Louise possessed all those qualities and virtues which could endear her to those who knew her intimately; but she lacked that air of familiarity which may be perfectly well combined with dignity, and is sufficient in France to captivate the crowd. One evening, when she had been at the Théâtre Français, Madame D—— ventured to tell her that the audience had been greatly disappointed, because, by remaining at the back of her box, she had deprived them of the privilege of seeing her.

" What matter?" said Madame de Montebello. " Why should her Majesty trouble herself?"

Madame D—— answered that a great number of people had gone to the theatre solely in the hope of seeing the Empress, that they had been very much annoyed at finding their expectation frustrated, and that her Majesty ought to regard their anxiety to see her as arising from a sentiment of affection always to be prized by a sovereign.

" When one is a frank and sincere person," said Madame de Montebello, " one should appear just what one is, and do nothing out of human respect."

With such advice as this always at hand, it is not surprising that the young Empress allowed her face and demeanour to betray to the public the weariness and distaste with which the duties imposed upon her by etiquette inspired her. Back again in her private life she was kindly, gentle, merry, affable, and beloved by all who were in habitual relations with her.

The first Empress had the advantage of possessing a thorough knowledge of the French character, and she availed herself of this to the fullest extent. No one had ever had so much influence over the mind of Napoleon, and even after her divorce she still retained a portion of it; so that Marie-Louise had conceived a sort of jealousy of her, and did not like any one to speak of Josephine in her presence. Josephine was renowned everywhere for her beneficence. Marie-Louise, too, was very charitable, but she allowed herself to be misled in the distribution of her gifts. In Josephine's time, Madame de Roche-foucauld, her Lady-in-Waiting, took charge of the distribution of the Empress's alms. She had employed two honest and respectable men to seek out the deserving poor who would not beg (*pauvres honteux*), and to collect trustworthy information respecting those who solicited her aid. A little money expended in this way restored a great number of families to life and happiness, and their gratitude spread the name of Josephine, with blessings upon it, throughout France. Marie-Louise took ten thousand francs a month from the sum allotted to her dress, for the poor; this was double what Josephine had given, but, unfortunately, Madame de Montebello regarded it as beneath her to occupy herself personally with the distribution of the money. She left it entirely to her secretary, who had formerly been valet-de-chambre to the Count d'Artois, and also secretary to Madame de Rochefoucauld. This person, however, had been nothing under the rule of Josephine's Lady-in-Waiting; he became all-powerful under that of Madame de Montebello.

He made a list on which the names of several poor persons were inscribed; it was then submitted to a kind of scrutiny; that is to say, M. Ballouhai, her Majesty's "secretary of expenditure," had inquiries made by a "sure" person into the statements

put forward by the applicants for relief, and returned
the list with notes to Madame de Montebello, who
handed it back to her secretary. The latter struck
out some of the names, inserted those of his favourites,
and took the revised list to the Duchess, who procured the Empress's signature to it. Thus altered,
it reached the hands of M. Ballouhai, who found
himself constrained to hand out the money while
lamenting over an abuse which he was powerless to
remedy. The names of immoral women figured in
the list; these were, however, mere pretences, and by
this means a portion of the Empress's alms remained
in the hands of M. Deluguy. Loud and frequent
complaints were raised against him, and also against
Madame de Montebello, but the echo of them never
reached the Empress. The Duchess had personal
knowledge of these malversations on several occasions, but her entire indifference to anything that
did not affect herself personally, blinded her to the
dishonesty of a man who was regarded with contempt by the public, and whom she ought over and
over again to have dismissed with ignominy.

One day, Marie-Louise, having visited the Jardin
des Plantes, desired Madame de Montebello to have
a present of 500 francs sent to the gardener, and the
Duchess's secretary received orders accordingly. A
few days afterwards, when the Duchess was walking
in the Jardin des Plantes with some other ladies,
the gardener approached the party and thanked

her for the 200 francs which she had sent him from
her Majesty. The secretary had thought proper to
appropriate the surplus. This theft was forgotten
like others, and thus it was that the poor were deprived of the succour which the Empress intended
them to receive, and herself of the blessings which
ought to have been its guerdon.

The almsgiving of Marie-Louise was not limited to
the fixed sum of 10,000 francs which she set aside
each month for the poor. No one ever spoke to
her of an unfortunate person, without arousing the
generous impulses, which sprang from her heart
at its first movement. Her second thoughts were
quite another matter; it was easy to discern a hidden
influence in their cold distrust and reluctance. From
other examples which I could give, I will select only
certain incidents that occurred under my own eyes.
One evening, just as the Empress had risen from
table and retired to the salon, a footman named
L'Espérance, a very respectable man, came in great
agitation to announce to a "first lady" that a family,
consisting of father, mother, and six children, living
on the seventh floor of a house in the Rue de L'Échelle,
had been entirely destitute of food for two days,
that, hearing of their condition, he had gone to investi-
gate it for himself, and was much grieved at having
no money wherewith to help in such an extremity.
The lady gave him twenty francs, and he took the
money at once to the starving family. When the

Empress returned the lady depicted to her the position
of these unfortunate people, and asked her for some
help for them. The Empress desired that 400 francs
should be taken to them on the spot, and when it was
represented to her that it was now near midnight, and
sufficient money had been sent to provide for their
wants until the morrow, she insisted, saying—

"No, no; some one must go to them. I am happy
to think that I shall make them pass a good night."

Some one did go, and that poor family was afterwards one of the objects of the Empress's bounty.

The following incident does Marie-Louise as much
honour as it does the Emperor himself.

The Countess de T——, a lady of the palace, one
day asked for audience of Napoleon, and her request
was granted without delay. She related to the
Emperor that her husband was in embarrassed
circumstances; that he was involved in law suits
which required heavy advances; that she counted on
his Majesty's kindness, and addressing herself, not to
the sovereign, but to the man, she said all sorts of
touching and tender things to him, without overstepping the bounds of that charming modesty which
so well becomes women, and of which the lady in
question was well known to make profession. Napoleon thanked her for having placed confidence in him,
assured her of his friendship, and on the spot signed
an order in her favour on his privy purse for 100,000
francs, payable at sight.

The Countess de T——, authorized by her husband, drew up a promissory note for the sum advanced in due form, and a year elapsed without its being possible to think of repaying it. At the end of that period the Countess gave birth to a son, and the Empress acted as godmother, selecting Prince Aldobrandini, her first equerry, as her fellow sponsor. Every one will have guessed what the christening present was. At the bottom of a magnificent casket (*corbeille*) lay the promissory note for 100,000 francs, receipted. But this was not all; the casket contained, besides, diamonds to the value of 12,000 francs, a superb Kashmir shawl, and some lace of the rarest beauty. It was like a fairy-tale! Let me hasten to add that the T—— family had rendered service to the State, and that those marks of favour, so gracefully conferred could not have been better bestowed, or have inspired more lively gratitude. A benefit, to be worthy of praise, must be bestowed on worthy, honourable persons.

The coldness of Marie-Louise's manner to all except her intimate friends was so well known that she was accused of extending it even to her son. This arose, however, not from want of affection, but from an excess of solicitude. She had never been with, or even seen, children, and she was afraid to take the little boy in her arms or caress him, lest she should do him some harm. Thus it came to pass that the young Napoleon became more attached to his governess than to his mother, and of this Marie-Louise promptly grew jealous. The Emperor, on the contrary, took him in his arms every time he saw him, caressed, and teased him, took him to a looking-glass and made all sorts of faces at him. At breakfast, he would keep the child in his lap, and, having dipped a finger in the sauce, make him suck it, or smear his face with it. The governess scolded, the Emperor laughed, and the child, who was almost always good-humoured, seemed to take pleasure in the rough play of his father. It may be observed that those who came at such times to the Emperor to solicit favours, were pretty sure to be graciously received, and to have their requests granted. The following anecdote supplies a case in point.

M. V——, a man of real talent, who was at once highly-informed and very poor, bethought him that he could fill a small salaried place quite as well as the dolts, great and small, who were so well paid under the Empire, and who had nothing on their side except good luck and their own importunity. He therefore asked for an appointment; but, having no patron, three or four petitions which he presented never reached the hands of the Emperor.

Worn out, impatient, and daily growing poorer, he devised a stratagem which would have been worthy of a courtier of Louis XIV. Necessity frequently inspires happy thoughts; he drew up with great care a little *placet* which he addressed to " His Majesty, the King of Rome." He only asked for a place worth

one hundred louis; this was a very modest request.
Full of the hope of success, he went to M. D——, a
superior officer who was aide-de-camp to the Emperor,
stated his distressful case, showed him the *placet*, and
added:

"General, you will again do a generous deed and
entitle yourself to my everlasting gratitude, if you
will procure me the means of presenting this request
to the Emperor."

M. D——, whose kindness was equal to his valour,
led the petitioner into the presence of Napoleon. His
Majesty took the paper, and remarked the superscrip-
tion with evident pleasure as well as surprise.

"Sire," said the applicant, "that is a petition for
His Majesty the King of Rome."

"Very well, then," replied the Emperor, "let it be
taken to its address."

The King of Rome was then six months old. A
Chamberlain was ordered to conduct the petitioner
into the presence of his baby Majesty. M. V——
seeing that fortune smiled upon him, was equal to the
occasion; he presented himself before the cradle of
the King, and, after he had made a profound and respectful reverence, he unfolded the paper, and read its
contents in a loud and distinct voice. The infant
King, having uttered some inarticulate sounds, M. V——
and the Chamberlain again saluted his Majesty and
returned to the Emperor, who asked, with the greatest
seriousness, what answer they had obtained.

"Sire," said the Chamberlain, "his Majesty, the King of Rome, made no reply."

"Very well," said Napoleon; "silence gives consent."

Shortly afterwards M. V—— was appointed to a post in a departmental administration with a salary of 6000 francs.

Before he was two years old the young Prince was regularly present at the Emperor's breakfast, and his mother also. Previous to her confinement, Marie-Louise had always breakfasted with the Emperor at a more or less fixed hour; but at that period Napoleon had resumed his former habit of eating when he was hungry, or when his occupations permitted, and he had insisted upon the Empress's continuing to breakfast at her usual hour.

No sooner could the little Napoleon speak, than he became, like almost all children, very inquisitive. The windows of his rooms looked out upon the garden and the courtyard of the Tuileries, and crowds of people assembled every day to see him. He took constant pleasure in watching them: and having remarked that a great many persons came into the palace with rolls of paper under their arms, he asked his governess the meaning of this. She told him that the bearers of the rolls were unfortunate persons who came to implore his papa's favour. From that time forth whenever he saw a petition being carried past he cried, sobbed, and could not be quieted, until it had

been brought to him; and every morning at breakfast
he presented to his father all those he had collected
the day before. As may be easily supposed, when this
became known to the public, the child was not allowed
to want petitions.

One day he saw under his window a woman in
mourning, holding by the hand a little boy of three
or four years old, also in mourning. The latter had
charge of a petition, which he held up from a distance
for the little Prince to see. The child wanted to know
" why that poor little boy was dressed all in black ? "
The governess answered that no doubt it was because
the little boy's papa was dead. He then urgently
begged to be allowed to speak to the child. Madame
de Montesquiou, who seized upon every opportunity
of developing his feelings for others, consented, and
directed that the little boy and his mother were to be
admitted. The mother was a widow, whose husband
had been killed in the last campaign, and she, being
destitute, had come to solicit a pension. The King of
Rome took the petition, and promised to give it to
his papa. On the following day he made up his parcel
as usual, but he kept the petition in which he took a
particular interest separate from the rest, and, having
handed over the others in a bundle, according to
custom, he said to the Emperor:

" Papa, here is a petition from a very poor little
boy. You are the cause of his father's death, and now
he has nothing. Give him a pension, I beg of you."

Napoleon took his son in his arms, kissed him tenderly, granted the pension, which he made retrospective, and had the patent made out that very day. Thus, to a child of three years old was granted the great privilege of drying the tears of a family.

It is an absolute falsehood that the young Prince was ever chastised with a rod. Madame de Montesquiou employed a much more wise and efficacious method of correcting his faults. He was generally docile, quiet, and amenable to reason, but occasionally he would give way to fits of passion. One day when he was rolling about on the floor, screaming, and would not listen to his governess, she closed the windows and the shutters. The child got up immediately, in great astonishment, and asked her what she did that for ?

"For fear you should be heard," she answered. "Do you think the French would have a Prince like you, if they knew you got into such passions ? "

"Do you think any one heard me ? " he asked. " I should be very sorry. Forgive me, *Maman Quiou*" (this was his name for her) ; " I will not do it any more."

Thus did a prudent and intelligent woman inspire the young Prince with the fear of blame, the respect for public opinion, so necessary in every rank, and endeavour to make the most of the good gifts and graces with which he was endowed by nature.

G

CHAPTER X.

FOR some time past a misunderstanding had existed
between France and Russia. France reproached
Russia with the violation of the continental system;
Russia claimed an indemnity for certain worthless
duchies that had been taken from the Empire, and
advanced some other pretensions. Russian forces
were massed, and approaching Warsaw, while a French
army was being formed at the same time in the north
of Germany; nevertheless, the idea of a war was as
yet far from being entertained.

These Cabinet mysteries, the unusual tone of some
of the confidential notes of 1811, the indication afforded
by great preparations secretly ordered, intrigues from
the outside, and hidden manoeuvres, aroused the suspicions of Russia. Already the Czar had seen that it
was time for him to find out the plans of Napoleon.

and, as he needed some other guarantee than that of
Kourakin, his ambassador, who was successfully
cajoled at Saint-Cloud, and an upholder of the continental system, he despatched Count Czernitschoff to
Paris, in the month of January, with a diplomatic
mission.

Count Czernitschoff, who was colonel of one of the
regiments of the Russian Imperial Guard, had attracted
attention at Napoleon's Court in the first instance
by his politeness, and his chivalrous language and
manners. He appeared at all the receptions and at
every fête, and achieved so striking a success in high
society, that he was very soon the fashion with
the ladies who were rivals for supremacy in grace
and beauty. Each of them aspired to the homage of
the brilliant and agreeable envoy of Alexander. At
first, he seemed to hesitate, but after a while this
Paris from the banks of the Neva accorded the apple
to the wife of General R——, who had recently
returned from the army in Spain.

The Minister of Police suspected that his stay in
Paris might have secret motives, and might conceal
a mystery which it would be well to penetrate;
accordingly he had the Count closely watched, and
learned that frequent interviews took place between
him and an under-secretary of the Ministry of War.
The Duke of Rovigo communicated his suspicions to
the Duke de Feltre, but was reassured by the latter,
who said he knew the intimacy was founded wholly

and solely upon their common taste for music, and need not give rise to any uneasiness. The vigilance of the police had not, however, been abated, when one day the Minister learned that the Colonel had left Paris quite suddenly on the preceding evening. He gave directions that the apartment which he had occupied should be carefully searched, and on this being done papers torn in very small pieces were found. These were brought to the Duke of Rovigo, who ordered his most skilful agents to put them together, and endeavour to decipher their contents. The thing was impossible, but the fact was ascertained that the torn papers had come out of one of the offices of the Ministry of War, which was indicated; it was the very office to which the suspected official belonged. The Duke of Rovigo went to the office at once, and in two hours' time he had ascertained that all the plans of campaign in Russia, the state of the forces, and the returns of our war material and means had been handed over to the Russian Colonel, who had departed for his own country, armed with these documents. Orders for his arrest were sent to the frontiers by telegraph, but when they reached Mayence, Czernitschoff had already passed through that city, and was out of reach. Many people believed that the Duke de Feltre was aware of the Colonel's real mission, and had favoured it secretly.

From the moment that Napoleon knew of Czernitschoff's departure, he considered war declared. For a long time past he had never allowed himself to be forestalled; he could march against Russia at the head of Europe, and his own destiny, as well as that of the new European system, would be decided by that conflict. Russia was the last resource of England; the peace of the globe was in Russia; the only thing to do was to go thither and secure it. Success ought not to be doubtful. Besides, he had always dreamed of achieving the independence of Poland; the opportunity had now arisen; he did not propose any gain to himself, he reserved for his own share only the glory of well doing, and the blessings of the future.

In the summer of that year the Emperor and Empress set out for Holland. Napoleon preceded Marie-Louise by two days, because he wished to visit the coasts of Belgium. They rejoined each other shortly afterwards, before making their entry into Amsterdam.

It was during this excursion that the first symptoms of the misunderstanding which had arisen between Napoleon and the Emperor of Russia began to be perceived. In the Empress's cabinet at Amsterdam a piano, constructed to look like a secretaire divided in two, with an empty space in the middle, had been placed. A small bust of the Emperor of Russia occupied this space. A few minutes after he arrived, the Emperor, who wanted to see what sort of accommo-

dation had been provided for the Empress, entered
the room, and perceiving the bust, took it up and put
it under his arm without saying a word. He went
through all the rooms, still carrying the bust, although
it was a good weight. When he had concluded his
tour of inspection, he handed the bust to Madame
D——, saying that he desired it should be removed.
This incident caused great surprise to all who
witnessed it; for we were yet far from supposing that
any misunderstanding between the two Emperors
existed.

Napoleon passed two months in visiting the ports
and principal cities, and came back to Brussels, where
his presence excited the greatest enthusiasm. By his
desire the Empress purchased one hundred and fifty
thousand francs' worth of lace, in order to revive the
national industry. The introduction of English merchandise into France was then strictly forbidden: all
the prohibited wares that were seized were burned
without mercy. The result was that every one was
trying to procure some of them. Belgium was still
full of English wares, carefully hidden, and all the
ladies in the suite of the Empress made large pur-
chases. Marie-Louise was not behindhand either.
Several vehicles were laden with these prizes, not
without fear lest the Emperor should be informed of
the fact, and should have them all seized on arriving
in France. The moment of departure came, the Rhine
was passed, and Coblenz reached. Fifteen vehicles,

bearing the arms of the Emperor, and composing the
first "service," or the advance guard, if I may use
that expression, arrived simultaneously at the gates
of the town. The officials were uncertain as to what
they ought to do; some wanted to stop and search
the vehicles, others were averse to doing so, alleging
that respect was due to everything belonging to the
Emperor. The latter counsels prevailed; the vehicles
entered freely, and having passed the first line of
the French customs they brought their cargo of prohibited merchandise to safe haven at Paris. It is quite
certain that if they had been stopped and confiscated,
Napoleon, far from taking it ill, would have laughed
heartily, and would probably have rewarded the individual who had been courageous enough to do his duty.

The Emperor had already definitely settled the
plan of his Russian expedition. He knew that such
a campaign would fail to obtain universal approbation, and it may have been solely with a view to
allaying the inevitable discontent that he now sought
to attach all hearts to him by exerting those powers
of pleasing with which he was richly endowed, but
did not always care to use.

He had never been known to be so affable, so
amiable; he made everybody welcome, and talked to
each comer on his own subjects. At Amsterdam he
was a banker, at Brussels a merchant, at Antwerp
a contractor and outfitter; he visited factories, in-
spected shipbuilding yards, reviewed the troops,

addressed speeches to the sailors, and attended the balls given for him in all the towns in which he made any stay. He was gracious and polite, he talked to everybody, and said nothing that was not pleasant.

Marie-Louise employed her brief sojourn at Amsterdam usefully. Her first visit was to the famous village of Bruck, situated about a league and a half from the city, and which communicates with the Zuyder Zee by means of a little canal, whose banks are enamelled with flowers at all seasons. She afterwards visited Saardam, celebrated for its historical connection with the memory of Peter the Great. Luncheon was served for the Imperial party in the hut that had been occupied by the autocrat of all the Russias, when learning practical ship-building.

It was while the Emperor and Empress were in Holland that Napoleon seemed to entertain a passing predilection for the Princess Aldobrandini, a young lady belonging to the Court, who had accompanied Marie-Louise. She was clever and amiable, and she talked remarkably well. One evening, when she had outshone her customary self, Napoleon said to the Empress and the Duchess of Montebello, that if they wished to become perfect they had only to try to copy the Princess. This was the first occasion on which he tried the temper of Marie-Louise. She expressed her annoyance only by silence, however, and showed no resentment towards the Princess. But the Duchess made it plain that she was deeply aggrieved, and from that time forth never ceased to say the hardest things of the favoured lady.

The electoral colleges had been assembled during the Emperor's absence, and a day or two after his return to Paris, Duroc, who had presided over that of the Department of the Meurthe, came to see Napoleon while he was at breakfast.

"Well," said the Emperor, "what do they think at Nancy of M. —— ?"

M. —— was one of the Emperor's chamberlains, and did not stand high in the favour of his master; but he had been born, and his property was situated, in the Department.

"Sire," replied the Marshal, "he is regarded with general esteem."

"That is not possible, Marshal; he is a fool."

"I beg your pardon, Sire; he is not a fool, but a man who is liked and esteemed because he deserves to be."

The Emperor laughed, and changed the conversation. He did not like to be contradicted, but he appreciated the courage of a man who, holding an opinion opposed to his own, ventured to maintain it boldly.

M. de Narbonne had also presided over an electoral college in a district at a distance from the capital.

"What do they say of me in the Departments through which you have passed?" asked the Emperor.

"Sire," replied M. de Narbonne, "some say you are a god, others say you are a devil; but all are agreed that you are more than a man."

Napoleon, not being altogether pleased with M. de Beauharnais, Gentleman-in-Waiting to Marie-Louise, had intended to appoint this same M. de Narbonne, who possessed ability and tact, in his place. The Duchess was afraid of M. de Narbonne, she preferred M. de Beauharnais, whom she had taken under her patronage, so she represented to the Empress that she ought to keep M. de Beauharnais with her, were it only for policy's sake, as, if his place were given to another person it would inevitably be reported everywhere that she had dismissed him on account of his name, and his relationship to Josephine. Marie-Louise believed her, and pleaded so hard with the Emperor that he at last consented to allow M. de Beauharnais to retain his place. To compensate M. de Narbonne for his disappointment, the Emperor made him his aide-de-camp.

Never was the Court of France more brilliant than during the winter that followed the visit to Holland. It was during fêtes and entertainments of every kind that Napoleon planned the conquest of Russia. The spoilt child of fortune, intoxicated with adulation, never contemplating the possibility of a reverse, seemed to be celebrating his future victories in anticipation, and to have called on all the Pleasures to aid the preparations for war. Not a day passed but there

was a play, a concert, or a masked ball at Court.
Nothing could exceed the brilliancy of these entertainments; the theatre especially was a dazzling
spectacle.

The Emperor and Empress occupied a box facing
the stage; on either side of them, and behind them,
sat the Princesses and Princes of their family; on the
right was the Foreign Ambassador's box; on the left
that of the French Ministers; all the rest of the first
tier of boxes, or rather the great gallery which was
substituted for it, was reserved for the Court ladies,
who attended in full dress and glittering with
diamonds. The pit was filled with men wearing
orders and stars of every kind; the second tier of
boxes was occupied by persons who had obtained
cards of admission; about one hundred cards were
distributed for each performance. Between the acts,
servants in the Emperor's livery went among the
whole audience, handing round ices and other refresh-
ments in profusion. The masked balls presented a
no less imposing spectacle in the richness and the
variety of costume. This sort of amusement was
particularly favoured by Napoleon: he never failed
to get information beforehand respecting the disguises
of the women whom he wanted to puzzle, and as he
was acquainted with all the scandalous stories, secret
intrigues, and general gossip of his Court, he took a
spiteful pleasure in tormenting the ladies, disturbing
the husbands, and alarming the lovers.

Before leaving Holland their Majesties visited Haarlem, the Hague, and Rotterdam; and after having crossed the Rhine, they visited Cologne. This was at the end of October, and the Imperial couple arrived at Saint Cloud early in November, 1811.

At that period, Madame Murat had induced the Emperor, by dint of importunity, to allow one of Lucien's daughters to be summoned to France. The young lady was residing with Madame Mère. Lucien had had two children by his first marriage, and five by the second, which Napoleon always refused to recognize. His refusal was founded upon the fact that his brother's second wife, the widow of a bankrupt "Agent de Change," retained and enjoined a fortune which was dishonestly withheld from her first husband's creditors.

Madame Murat's object in sending for Lucien's daughter was to make her Queen of Spain. This feat, indeed, appeared perfectly easy of accomplishment. The Princes were at Valençay, and Ferdinand, whose letters to the Emperor were all of the most flattering kind, begged as a favour that he would bestow the hand of one of his kinswomen upon him. The resistance of the Spaniards had made Napoleon come to the resolution of replacing Ferdinand on the throne, and giving him his niece in marriage. The Princess was a fine handsome girl; I often saw her with the Empress. All of a sudden we learned that she had been sent back to her father. It was said that the cause of this peremptory step was a letter, written by the Princess to Lucien, in which the Emperor and Empress were not too tenderly handled. The imprudent communication was intercepted and placed before the Emperor, who at once dismissed his niece from Court.

CHAPTER XI.

NAPOLEON AND HIS COURT AT DRESDEN.

DEPARTURE FROM SAINT CLOUD—ARRIVAL AT DRESDEN—THE EMPEROR
AND EMPRESS OF AUSTRIA—NAPOLEON'S ANCESTRAL NOBILITY
THE KING OF PRUSSIA AND HIS SON—FÊTES AND THEATRICAL
ENTERTAINMENTS—MADAME TALMA—THE EMPEROR ALEXANDER—
NAPOLEON SETS OUT FOR POLAND—THE JOURNEY OF MARIE-LOUISE
TO PRAGUE—HER RETURN TO SAINT CLOUD.

NAPOLEON left Saint Cloud on the 9th of May, 1812.
Marie-Louise and her husband occupied the same
carriage. A portion of the Court and almost the whole
of their Majesties' household accompanied them on
this journey. Never did a departure to join an army
so closely resemble a party of pleasure. We arrived
at Mayence on the 11th of May; the Emperor at once
reviewed the troops and then proceeded to inspect all
the neighbouring strongholds. On the 13th we
stopped at Aschaffenburg, at the residences of the
Prince Primate and the Grand Duke, the Empress's
uncle, where the King of Wurtemberg and the Grand
Duke of Baden already were. On the 16th their
Majesties were met at Fribourg by the King and

Queen of Saxony, who were impatient to welcome the illustrious travellers; and on the same day, at ten o'clock in the evening, Napoleon and Marie-Louise arrived at Dresden.

The Emperor and Empress occupied the state apartments of the château, and were constantly surrounded by a number of their own household. Napoleon's levee took place as usual at eight o'clock. It was then and there that the world might have beheld with wonder the submissiveness of a multitude of kings and princes, mixing with a crowd of courtiers of all sorts, and awaiting the moment at which they might present themselves before him. On the day after his arrival the Emperor's levee was attended by the reigning Princes of Saxe-Weimar, Saxe-Coburg, and Nassau. The King of Westphalia and the Grand Duke of Wurtzberg arrived during the day, and immediately paid their respects to him.

On the 18th, the Emperor and Empress of Austria made their state entry into Dresden. What a moment for Marie-Louise! Once more to find herself in the arms of her father, and to reappear before the dazzled eyes of her family as the happiest of wives and the consort of the greatest of sovereigns! Her august father could not conceal his emotion; he tenderly embraced his son-in-law, and recognizing the claim to his affection that Napoleon had acquired, he emphatically assured him that he might count upon him and upon Austria for the triumph of the common cause.

At their first interview, the Emperor of Austria informed Napoleon that the Buonaparte family had formerly been sovereign at Treviso; of this fact he was sure, because he had caused the authentic titles to be procured and presented to him. He attached so much importance to the proof of Napoleon's nobility that he left the Emperor abruptly in order to communicate the good news to Marie-Louise, who was also greatly delighted to hear it.

On that day the King of Saxony gave a magnificent banquet to all these illustrious guests. The principal ministers, the confidants, and the private advisers of the sovereigns and the princes crowded in behind them; among the number were Metternich and Hardenberg. Their attitude in the presence of Napoleon was that of profound admiration for his genius; their language, in conversation with the members of the imperial household, was that of devotion to his person.*

The King of Prussia was not present at this great assembly. It had been arranged that if Napoleon should leave Dresden to join the army he was to pass through Berlin, where, indeed, preparation had already been made for him, and the King of Prussia remained in his capital to receive him. Nevertheless on the 26th the King arrived at Dresden, and hastened to visit Napoleon, to whom he said:—

* A significant commentary upon this passage, and indeed upon the famous banquet at Dresden, and the protestations of the Emperor of Austria, is supplied by the Talleyrand Correspondence during the Congress of Vienna (Bentley).—Translator's note.

"Sire, my brother, I repeat to you my assurance of inviolable attachment to the system which unites us."

He offered Napoleon the services of his son, the Crown Prince of Prussia, in the capacity of aide-de-camp in the campaign upon which he was about to enter. His Prussian Majesty even presented the Prince to the aides-de-camp of the Emperor of the French, begging their friendship for this new brother in arms. But, no sooner had the first fervour of the occasion subsided than comparisons, jealousies, and animosities crept in and established themselves, so that when the Princes and Princesses parted, each to return home, they were on less friendly terms than they had intended to be, or at least than they had been before the great meeting.

I shall not attempt to describe the grandeur of that Court, whither so many Courts had come from the farthest parts of Germany, and the luxury in which each rivalled the other,—fêtes, concerts, balls, hunting-parties, assemblies, competing with each other for their respective share in the whirl of pleasure. Incessant movement and animation turned the Saxon capital into an abode of dazzling magnificence, whose centre was Napoleon.

In order to give the inhabitants of Dresden an idea of the splendour which surrounded his throne, the Emperor of the French had brought with him all that could contribute to its adornment. The theatre had

H

not been neglected. Among his suite were the principal members of the Comédie Française. Of course, Talma had not been forgotten. He brought his wife with him, in the hope of effecting a reconciliation between her and the Emperor, who could not endure her (I do not know why), while he loaded her husband with tokens of his favour and generosity. Talma did not succeed. When the object of his unjust dislike appeared, he plainly showed his displeasure, and ordered his Prefect of the Palais to signify to Madame Talma that she was not again to show herself upon the French stage.

Napoleon was very busy at Dresden, and Marie-Louise, ever anxious to take advantage of the few leisure moments which her husband could spare her, hardly went out at all lest she might miss any of them. The Emperor Francis, who did nothing, and was excessively bored, could not understand this domestic seclusion, and amused himself, as a last resource, in walking about the town all day and haunting the shops. The Empress of Austria tried to make Marie-Louise do the same, telling her that her assiduity was ridiculous. She would have followed the lead of her step-mother, if she had not been afraid of Napoleon. It was his wish that his wife should display the utmost magnificence on this occasion. All the Crown Jewels had been taken to Dresden; Marie-Louise was literally covered with them; and the Empress of Austria, who had done her very utmost to

make a splendid appearance, was mortified to find
herself eclipsed by her step-daughter. She used to
come in almost every morning while Marie-Louise was
dressing, and ferret about everywhere ; rummaging
the Empress's laces, ribbons, stuffs, shawls, trinkets,
etc., etc., and she never went away empty-handed.
She hated Napoleon; in vain did he employ all
the resources of French gallantry to overcome her
dislike. He never could triumph over the inveterate
aversion which she frequently, but unconsciously,
allowed to appear.

The meeting at Dresden was the high-water
mark of Napoleon's power. He had to show that he
desired to have a little more made of the Emperor of
Austria, his father-in-law, than was actually done.
Neither the Emperor, nor the King of Prussia, had a
house allotted to his suite. All ate at Napoleon's
table, and it was he who settled the hours, the
etiquette, and the *ton*. When he made the Emperor
Francis or the King of Prussia go before him, these
sovereigns were highly pleased. The luxury and magnificence of the Court of France caused Napoleon to be
regarded as an Eastern King might have been. There,
as at Tilsit, he distributed profuse gifts of money and
diamonds. During his stay at Dresden. he had not
a single French soldier about his person; his only
escort was formed of the Saxon body-guard.

The Emperor Alexander had arrived at Wilna at
the end of April, accompanied by all his Staff, and

from thence he had made his entry into the capital of
Poland. Stress of circumstances, therefore, obliged
Napoleon to send an ambassador to the Czar without
delay. He selected, for this important mission, the
Archbishop of Malines (Mechlin), who started at once,
accompanied by M. de Narbonne, then aide-de-camp
to the Emperor. He saw Alexander, and found him
firm in the resolution which he had formed, if the
indemnities which he had previously demanded
through Kourakin, his ambassador, were not granted.
In consequence, Napoleon prepared to leave Dresden.
On the 28th he made all his arrangements with the
Secretaries of State despatched from Paris to Dresden
by the various Ministers, and the next day at two
o'clock a.m., he left the Saxon capital to place himself at the head of the finest army he had yet commanded. The Prince of Neufchatel occupied a place
in his carriage, the Grand Marshal and the Grand
Equerry followed close behind; the rest of his civil
and military household had already preceded him.
The Duke of Bassano and Count Daru remained at
Dresden in order to forward despatches, while awaiting
the Emperor's commands to rejoin him.

No sooner was Napoleon gone than all the Princes
hastened to return to their own realms. For the first
time Marie-Louise beheld the crowd ebb away from
before her. The only one who remained with her was
her uncle, the Grand Duke of Wurtzberg. On the 5th
of June, the Empress herself set out for Prague. The

Emperor and Empress of Austria came to meet her with all their Court. Her Majesty left her own carriage and seated herself in her father's. The entry of the brilliant *cortège* into the city of Prague was made amid the roar of cannon and the ringing of bells; the streets were lined with troops, and all the houses were magnificently draped.

On arriving at her apartments in the Palace, her Majesty found all the civil, religious, and military authorities of the city assembled, together with such personages as had not taken part in the *cortège*, and a numerous "service of honour" selected by the Emperor of Austria from among the most distinguished members of his household.

On the 18th of June, Marie-Louise returned to Saint Cloud from Prague.

CHAPTER XII.

DEPARTURE OF NAPOLEON TO JOIN THE ARMY—THE MARCH UPON MOSCOW
—THE CONSPIRACY OF MALLET—THE EMPEROR'S WORDS—THE DUKE
OF ROVIGO—DISASTERS—NAPOLEON'S RETURN TO PARIS—THE PRAYER
OF THE KING OF ROME—PREPARATIONS FOR A FRESH CAMPAIGN—
THE DUKE DE FELTRE.

NAPOLEON had set out for Poland, whither he was
summoned by a people who believed that he was
about to re-establish the kingdom, and restore its
former boundaries. He did nothing of the kind; his
views were of a different nature, and this was an
error which cost him dear. He marched at the
head of the finest army that France had ever raised,
reinforced by auxiliary troops from Italy and the con-
federation of the Rhine, and provided with formidable
parks of artillery and immense stores.

At first victory seemed disposed to remain faithful
to him who had hitherto been its favourite, and he
marched on from success to success, so far as Smolensk.
Having reached that town, he was a while disposed to
advance no farther; he talked of this project to his
confidants, and alluded to the region at which he had
arrived as a *barbarous country*. But one of his
generals pointed out to him, that, as he had often

signed treaties of peace in capitals, he was bound to go on to Moscow, in order there to sign the peace with Russia. He hearkened to this imprudent counsel, and set out on his march towards the ancient capital of the Czars.

When the Emperor arrived at Moscow, where he expected to get provisions for his troops, and to be able to give them some rest, he found the city burning, and no supplies for his army. He wrote to the Emperor Alexander, proposing to treat with him for peace. Several days elapsed before Alexander arrived at any decision; but at length he wrote to the General in command of his army to the effect that he would consent to treat for peace with Napoleon. At the moment when the Czar's orders reached the Russian head-quarters, Moscow was in flames, and the cold had already set in with great intensity. The General took it upon himself to defer the execution of his Sovereign's commands, being convinced that the French army would be forced to retire, and that the Emperor would be well pleased with his disobedience. He was right; the misfortunes of the French army were directly caused by that act.*

While Napoleon was returning from Moscow, an extraordinary event was occurring in Paris.† A

---

* This circumstance was communicated to the author by a Russian nobleman who was perfectly acquainted with the facts.

† It was at Smolensk, and during the disastrous retreat, that Napoleon was suddenly informed of the famous exploit of General Mallet. The following account of the incident is taken from Ségur's

person who had escaped from prison seized the
Minister of Police, threw him into a dungeon, made

Histoire de Napoléon et de la Grande Armée, pendant l'année 1812,
vol. ii. ch. xii. :—

"We were on the heights of Mikalewka, on the 6th of November,
and the sleet-laden clouds had just discharged themselves upon our
heads, when we saw Count Daru coming up in haste, and a circle of
vedettes was formed around him and the Emperor.

"An estafette, the first who had been able to reach us for ten days
past, had just brought the news of that strange conspiracy, formed in
Paris by an obscure general in confinement. His only accomplices
were the false news of our destruction, and forged orders to some
troops to arrest the Minister, the Prefect of Police, and the Commandant of Paris. The success of all this was due to the impulse of a
first movement, and the general ignorance and astonishment. But no
sooner had the first rumour of it been spread than an order sufficed
to consign the head of the conspiracy to prison once more, with his
accomplices or his dupes.

"The Emperor was informed simultaneously of their crime and their
punishment. Those who tried from a distance to read his thoughts
in his face saw nothing. He was absolutely reticent; his first and
only words to Daru were: 'Well! and if we had stayed at Moscow!'
Then he hastily entered a palisaded house which was used as a post
of correspondence. No sooner was Napoleon alone with his most
faithful and trusted officers than all his emotions broke out at once in
exclamations of astonishment, humiliation, and anger. A few minutes
later, he sent for several officers in order to ascertain the effect that
had been produced by such strange news. He detected in them all
distress, uneasiness, even consternation, and perceived that confidence
in the stability of his government was shaken. He also came to know
that his officers accosted each other with lamentation, and were agreed
that the great revolution of 1789, which was supposed to be ended, was
still active.

"Some persons were rejoiced at the news, hoping that it would
hasten the Emperor's return to France, and that he would remain
there, not exposing himself to risks from the outside, because he was
no longer sure of the inside. As for Napoleon, all his thoughts had
preceded him to Paris, and he continued to advance mechanically
towards France; but he had no sooner arrived than he summoned the
Grand-Chancellor to Saint Cloud, and, advancing towards him the
moment he caught sight of him, his eyes blazing with anger, he

himself master of the military post, and was on the point of overturning the Imperial Government in a few hours. This attempt was badly conducted, but the moment could not have been better chosen. The war with Russia had occasioned almost general discontent; the new levies of men which it had necessitated turned all classes against it.

It was actually hoped that Napoleon might not obtain too great a success, because the general conviction was, that if he did he would afterwards despatch troops by land to endeavour to destroy the English power in India. This appeared to be the real aim of his desires and his ambition. His absence, at so great a distance, made people talk and murmur more freely. The Ministers inspired but little fear. All things therefore seemed to unite to favour a conspiracy.

At this moment Mallet, a general who was suspected by the Emperor, and shut up in an asylum on the pretext of madness, conceived the project of a revolution, and proceeded to put it into execution, without any settled plan, and without either accomplices or money. Having escaped from the house where he was confined, and provided himself with forged decrees of the Senate, which announced the death of the Emperor, and appointed General Mallet to the Military Command of Paris, he went alone, in the middle of

addressed him in a voice of thunder: 'Ah, so you have come, sir! Who gave you leave to have my officers shot? Why have you deprived me of the fairest of a sovereign's rights, the right to pardon? Sir, you are very culpable!'"—Communicated note.

the night, to a barrack, read out the so-called decree
of which he was the bearer, and ordered a regiment
to follow him. From thence he repaired to the prison
of La Force, and in virtue of the dignity with which
he had invested himself, he ordered the release of
a general officer, named Lahorie, who had been im-
prisoned on some police charge, and on whom he
believed he could rely. The latter, with a detachment of the same regiment, proceeded to the hotel
of the Minister of Police, informed him of the death
of Napoleon, and, also, that he had the commands
of the Senate to secure the Minister's person. The
Duke of Rovigo, only half awake, surrounded on
all sides, and stunned by the double intelligence,
allowed himself to be arrested and taken to La Force.
Before seven o'clock in the morning, he was under
lock and key in the same prison from which Lahorie
had been released a few hours before, and he was very
soon joined by the Prefect of Police, who had also
allowed himself to be arrested with equal credulity.

During this time, Mallet had gone to the staff-
quarters of the Place de Paris, in order to arrest
General Hulin; but the latter was not so confiding
as Savary. He asked to see the decree of the Senate,
and Mallet, pretending to take it out of his pocket,
drew a pistol, fired at the general and broke his jaw.
At that moment, Adjutant-General Laborde, an active
and dauntless man, arrived.

On being informed of what had occurred, he convinced the officers who had followed Mallet that they were the dupes of an impostor, and seized upon him. Laborde then proceeded to the Ministry of Police, and there he found Lahorie, who, after having given the clerks orders to draw up a circular despatch, was in serious consultation with a tailor from whom he was ordering a coat. Laborde had him arrested, and then went on to La Force to release the Minister of Police. Lastly, having repaired to the department, he found another emissary sent by Mallet, and the Prefect, who was as credulous as Rovigo, busily engaged in the preparation of a room in which the provisional Government was to meet in the course of the morning. By eleven o'clock order had been restored everywhere.

Marie-Louise was at Saint Cloud while all this was taking place in Paris. It must be said, to her honour, that she showed coolness and courage on the occasion. She commanded the few troops at the palace to place themselves under arms; but this was barely done when she learned that the conspirators had been arrested.

The news of the alleged death of the Emperor, and the authentic intelligence of the arrest of the Minister and the Prefect of Police, had spread rapidly through Paris without producing any effect. There was no manifestation of joy, nor was there any sign of grief. The faubourgs of Saint Antonio and Saint Marceau, which had been, respectively, such centres of agitation in all our revolutions, remained perfectly quiet. The only

sentiment by which the Parisians seemed to be
animated was that of a spectator watching a game
of dominoes—curiosity to know how all this would
end. The next day no more was thought about it,
except as it furnished an opportunity for sarcastic
observations upon the Minister of Police, of whom it
was said, among other things, that on the present
occasion he had made a *tour de force.*

While I am on the subject of the Mallet conspiracy, I must relate an anecdote which does honour
to the unfortunate Lahorie. A year before the time
of which I am speaking, he had been sentenced to be
shot. Savary, who had known him formerly, managed
to save his life. At the moment when the arrest of
the Duke was attempted, a sergeant in command of
a portion of troops accompanying Lahorie, wanted to
kill him. Lahorie rushed upon the sergeant, whom
he disarmed, and declared that as the Duke had saved
his life, nobody should touch him. Savary did what
he could, after the event, to prevent the condemnation
of Lahorie, and, having failed, he took special care of
his family.

As I have alluded to the Duke of Rovigo, I shall
relate a few particulars which ought to modify the
unfavourable impression of his character that has
been produced by certain libellous publications.

His father, a former lieutenant-colonel of the Royal
Normandy Regiment of Cavalry, placed his son, then
sixteen years of age, in that regiment, in 1789. The

young man was aide-de-camp to General Ferino for
five years and a half; his good looks, and his gallantry in the war, had procured that post for him.
He lost it on the 18th Fructidor, but served
General Desaix in a similar capacity, accompanying
him to Egypt and returning with him. On the death
of the General, he became aide-de-camp to Napoleon.

His great activity and exactitude rendered him
a favourite with his superior officers; he was very
ambitious and had a thirst for success; his manners
were rough, his tone was overbearing, but he had
natural ability and great self-devotion. He said that
when the Emperor was in question, he knew neither
wife nor children; this was the very fanaticism of
gratitude.*

It is due to him to state that he never slighted
any of his former friends.

All the officers of the Royal Normandy Regiment,
whether *émigrés* or not, who wanted places, had only
to apply to him. He got a prefectship for his former
colonel. I could quote two hundred persons who have
owed their means of livelihood to him.

When he was Minister of Police he was constantly
exposed to much that was very unpleasant in consequence of his patronage of certain persons. The

* No doubt this saying of Savary's gave rise to the calumny
previously referred to by the writer, and which imputed to Napoleon the
observation that he "liked Savary because he would shoot his father if
he (the Emperor) desired him to do so."—Translator's note.

two Polignacs, for instance, owe the many and great alleviations of their captivity to him.

While these events were taking place, Napoleon had arrived at Moscow, and had seen the city burned by the Russians, so that the French might not profit by the provisions, the munitions, and the wealth of all kinds which it contained. Alexander kept his enemy amused by proposals of peace, because he was reckoning upon a powerful auxiliary, which could not fail to come to his aid, and was bound to be much more fatal to the French troops than all his own forces combined. Wise men feared and foresaw great misfortunes, but the Emperor would not listen to any advice. How could he make up his mind to retrace his steps without having struck a decisive blow? At last, Prince Poniatowski spoke out to him.

"Sire," said he, "your army is incurring the greatest danger. I know the climate; the weather is fine to-day, the thermometer stands at 4° (Réaumur), but it may fall this very evening to 20° and 30."

Napoleon yielded, and gave the order for departure on the next day but one. On the morrow, however, the event predicted by Prince Poniatowski came to pass. The disasters which followed are well known. The French army was completely destroyed; those whom hunger, cold, or the Russian steel spared, were sent as prisoners to the depths of Siberia.

The Emperor made his retreat, if indeed the name of retreat can be given to a precipitate flight; for he did not pause once until he had reached Saxon territory.

The celebrated bulletin, drawn up by Napoleon himself, which allowed a great part of our vast misfortune to be discerned, without, however, making known its full extent, was received at Paris. All France was plunged into consternation; there was hardly a family which had not either to mourn or to fear.

Napoleon did not pause in Saxony; he immediately resumed his journey to France. He had written to the Empress several times, but without announcing his return, and he arrived unexpectedly. Marie-Louise, who had been for some time very ailing and depressed, had just retired to rest; Mademoiselle K——, who slept in the room adjoining her Majesty's, was preparing to do likewise, and about to close all the approaches, when she heard voices in the salon beyond. At the same moment the door opened, and two men, wearing heavy furred cloaks, entered the room. She rushed to the door of the Empress's room, to bar their approach, when, one of the two men having thrown off his cloak, she recognized the Emperor. A cry uttered by her had apprised the Empress that something extraordinary was occurring in the next room, and she was just getting out of her bed when the Emperor came in and clasped her in his arms. The interview was a tender one. Napoleon's companion was M. de Caulaincourt, who had come with him to the palace in

a shabby caléche. So little were they expected, that
they had great difficulty in getting the gates opened
to admit them.

There was less gaiety at Court that winter than
during the last. The entertainments were few, and
pleasure seemed to be banished from them. For some
time Napoleon was gloomy and absent-minded; he was
reluctant to show himself in public, and seemed to fear
that he would be badly received. In this he was mistaken, and the public proved to him that he had mis-
judged them. He appeared, indeed, in a new light; he
was no longer the ever-victorious hero : for the first
time they beheld him unfortunate and a fugitive. His
errors were blamed, the losses we had suffered were
bitterly deplored; but interest in him, affection for him,
were re-awakened by the sight of him, and loud accla-
mations greeted him, not of the purchased sort, but
coming from the heart. The French are eminently
generous; they proved it on this occasion. Even those
who loved him not kept silence, and refrained from
insulting him in a misfortune which so many brilliant
memories entitled them to regard as merely temporary.

This reception emboldened him; and having already
resolved to form a new army without delay, he sought
to make himself popular, because he knew that no
sacrifice is too costly for the French, when it is made
for a prince whom they love. He went out much
more in public, visited all the institutions and public
works, accompanied only by a single aide-de-camp,

talked familiarly with all whom he met, and distributed tokens of his generosity on all sides. He
sometimes met with people who ventured to ask him
for "peace." To them he would reply that peace was
the object of his most ardent desire; that France
had won sufficient glory by her arms; and that he
purposed to make only one more campaign, in order
to place the tranquility of the Empire upon a sound
and solid basis.

Madame de Montesquiou, who was anxious to inspire her charge from his infancy with those principles
of piety which were so remarkable in herself, had
accustomed the King of Rome to pray to God night and
morning. After the disasters of the Russian campaign,
she taught him to add the following words to his
childish prayer—"Inspire, O Lord God, my papa with
the desire to make peace, for the welfare of France and
of us all." One evening, Napoleon was in his son's
room. The time came for the child to say his prayers;
Madame de Montesquiou made no change in them, and
the Emperor heard the little King of Rome repeat the
words which I have just quoted. He smiled, but said
nothing. Napoleon was aware of the sentiments of
Madame de Montesquiou; she had already had the
courage to tell him what his flatterers sought to
conceal from him,—the great need and the desire of
France for peace. He listened to her calmly, answered
that he *wanted to* make peace, and then changed the
conversation.

I

In the mean time preparations for this fresh campaign went on with incredible activity. New arms seemed to fall from the sky; immense magazines of provisions, forage, and munitions were formed; and men rose apparently from the earth to fill up the roster of the former regiments or to form new ones, which passed in succession before the Emperor. One day, as he was looking at a newly formed regiment of Chasseurs defiling under the windows of the Tuileries, he cried, " What a fine regiment ! With that one may be sure of conquering every one and everywhere."

The formation of the Guards of Honour excited against him all the old nobles and all the rich people, who had paid considerable sums to shield their sons from the obligation of military service by purchasing substitutes for them : many persons had been obliged to do this twice and even three times over. The measure was so unjust and so impolitic, that many people suspected the Duke de Feltre, who proposed it, of the perfidious intention of turning against the Emperor that class which, although it was the least numerous, was the most to be feared, on account of its talents, its wealth, and its influence. In short, it was believed that the Minister had been suborned by some foreign power.

The Duke de Feltre (Clarke) had also behaved in a suspicious way with respect to the conspiracy, or, as it ought rather to be called, the ill-concerted enterprise of General Mallet. He asserted that he had given

orders to have Mallet arrested, and that he had
mounted his horse and ridden through the streets of
Paris in order to quiet and undeceive the public mind.
It is quite true that he did all this, but not until after
Laborde had arrested Mallet and taken the Duke of
Rovigo out of La Force. Until then he had remained
quietly in his house, and he appears to have waited
until the whole thing was over before making any
movement.

CHAPTER XIII.

NAPOLEON by no means deceived himself with regard
to the crisis with which France was threatened;
he clearly discerned the immensity of his peril, when
he opened the campaign. Ever since his return from
Moscow, he had fully recognized the danger of the
situation, and applied himself to averting it. Thenceforth he had made up his mind to the greatest sacrifices; but the moment at which he should acknowledge this was a difficulty with which his mind was
especially occupied.

The fidelity of the allies of France in Germany did
not yet appear to be shaken; nevertheless, he already
entertained doubts of the good faith of Austria, and he
imparted them to the Duke of Bassano, Minister of
Foreign Affairs, who, notwithstanding his intelligence

and finesse, was the last man who ought to have been placed in that important position, as he had been more than once duped by foreign Cabinets. Being questioned by the Emperor upon the dispositions of Austria, he assured him in the most positive way that they were entirely pacific and amicable. It appears, indeed, that the Minister, either credulous or deceived, was sincerely persuaded of this, and induced Napoleon to share his conviction. Marie-Louise, who trembled lest the union which had existed between her father and her husband should be broken, was grateful to the Emperor for the way in which he was acting, and for his confidence in the fidelity of the Emperor of Austria. She had not liked the Duchess of Bassano, but from that moment she took her into her good graces, and on every occasion lavished tokens of regard upon her. The Court was surprised to see the Duchess promoted to such favour all of a sudden, and attributed the fact to the intimacy which existed between her and Madame de Montebello. But every one was mistaken; the real cause was that which I have just indicated.

In the middle of spring the Emperor set out for the north of Germany, whither he had already despatched his troops. Before his departure, he appointed the Empress Regent of the Empire, and his brother Joseph President of the Council of Regency. Marie-Louise accompanied him so far as Mayence. On seeing the troops it was indeed difficult to believe that they could have been furnished by a nation which had just lost so numerous an army in the preceding campaign.

On the 2nd of May Napoleon opened the campaign of Saxony by the victories of Lutzen and Bautzen. But those victorious days were days of mourning for him: Bessières, Duke of Istria; Bruyère, General of the Guard; and Duroc, the Grand Marshal, lost their lives. The Emperor was sincerely attached to all three. He felt the loss of Duroc more keenly than that of the others, owing to their old friendship and the associations common to both.

Some details of Duroc's death may be acceptable. Those which I am about to relate, were communicated to me by an eye-witness of the event in whom I have entire confidence, and who remained with Duroc until he had ceased to breathe.

The Emperor did not arrive at his head-quarters until the 20th of May, at nine o'clock in the evening.

"Every day has its troubles," said he to the principal officers of his army who surrounded him; "let us give a few moments to rest, and we will begin again to-morrow."

He then sat down to his modest repast, and remarking the presence of his first Comptroller, M. Colin, he said to him with a smile, "Ha! ha! are you there, Monsieur le brave?" Turning to the Prince of Neufchâtel, he added, "This devil of a fellow actually came to look for me this morning in the midst of the

battle to give me a crust of bread and a glass of wine !
It was not a very convenient place, was it, Colin ?
You will remember that breakfast."

" Yes, Sire," muttered the faithful servant between
his teeth ; " and especially the bombshells that were
dancing about your Majesty."

The next day—a day of battle—the Emperor kept
at the heels of the vanguard. The bullets whistled
like a hailstorm around him, and he could not conceal
his vexation on seeing the enemy's army constantly
escaping him.

" What !" said he, "no result after such butchery ?
Not a prisoner ! These people will not leave so much
as a nail behind them !"

At that moment one of his escort, a Chasseur of
the Guides, was killed by a Russian bullet. Napoleon,
who saw him fall almost under his horse's feet, said,
addressing his Grand Marshal, " Duroc, fortune has
a spite against us to-day."

The day was not ended.

The Emperor, perceiving a height from whence he
could see what was passing, galloped rapidly down
the hollow in order to regain a narrow way which
led to it.   He was accompanied by the Duke of
Vicenza, the Duke of Treviso, Marshal Duroc, and
General Kirgener of the Engineers ; all following at
a quick trot and close together. At that moment the
enemy fired three cannon shots ; one of the balls struck
a tree close to the Emperor, and ricochetted. Napoleon,

having reached the plateau which overlooked the ravine, turned round to ask for his field-glass, and saw nobody but the Duke of Vicenza, who had followed him.   Duke Charles of Placenza came up soon afterwards and whispered something to the Grand Equerry. The Emperor asked what it was.

"Sire," said the Duke of Vicenza, "the Grand Marshal has been killed."

"Duroc!" exclaimed the Emperor. "Bah! that is not possible; he was beside me just now."

On this, the page on duty came up with the glass; he was as pale as death, and he confirmed the sad news. He had seen the ball ricochet from the tree and strike, first General Kirgener, and then the Duke of Friula.

"Kirgener was killed on the spot, but the Grand Marshal is not yet dead; and your Majesty's glass has escaped," added the page, with a forced smile.

During this time the doctors, Larrey and Ivan, had hurried up, but they could do nothing; the intestines had been torn by the ball.

All the army participated in the grief which absorbed Napoleon. The old Grenadiers said, as they fixed their eyes upon him, "Poor man! that one was an *intime!*"

The news that his Grand Marshal had ceased to suffer, which was brought to him in the morning, did more to turn his thoughts from his sorrow than even the tortuous manœuvres of the enemy. Some time after this event, the Emperor said to one of his generals that he had lost at Bautzen, in the most stupid way in the world, the three men whom he liked best and esteemed still more ; Bruyère, Bessières, and Duroc. The three were killed on the same day by three trifling cannonades.

The battle of Leipsic was fought a few days afterwards, and was followed by the desertion of the Emperor by his allies. Napoleon was obliged to leave Germany as precipitately as he had fled from Russia, and was only enabled to reach Mayence by the noble self-devotion of his Guard, who were cut to pieces in covering his retreat.

The Regent wrote frequently to the Emperor, and did not conceal the state of feeling in Paris and the provinces, where all desired peace and loudly demanded it.

We had just received the news of some slight successes, and a glimmering of hope had been re-awakened at Court, when two wretched hack carriages arrived at Saint Cloud. The Emperor was recognized, and his unexpected return at once revealed that he had to announce fresh disasters. The Empress was with her son. Some one went to tell her ; she ran to meet her husband, who was coming up the steps of the palace, and threw herself into his arms in a flood of tears. Napoleon, deeply moved, clasped her to his heart with the utmost tenderness, and their little son, who was brought down by his governess, added the last touch to a family picture, which was deeply interesting to the small number of spectators who witnessed it.

The Empress, aware of the conduct of Austria, dreaded the return of the Emperor almost as much as she desired it. He was calm, resigned, and did not yet despair of his fortunes, but applied himself to calculate the resources which still remained to him. Above all, he did not show the slightest disposition to hold his wife responsible for the faithlessness of her father.

There was no longer any question of carrying the war into distant lands, of making conquests, of destroying ancient monarchies, or of founding new ones ; the pressing matter was to prevent the foreigner from penetrating into the heart of France, and to maintain the integrity of her territory, so as to secure the safety of the Imperial crown, which was now in danger of falling from the head of Napoleon. To do this he must create a new army for the second time ; procure arms, munitions, horses, victuals, money, and above all, men. The measures which were adopted were equivalent to the former convocation of the *ban*, and the *arrière-ban*.

At the mention of the fresh forces the general discontent reached its height, and although it did not break out into sedition, it found utterance in murmurs, and the orders of the Government were executed slowly and only in part. The Chamber of representatives was summoned, and the deputies appeared there to give voice to the feelings and wishes of their constituents, who had everywhere declared for peace. Napoleon's reverses had restored some courage to the friends of liberty. The Senate persisted in the system of base flattery which had degraded it in the eyes of all Europe, but the Legislative Body exhibited more spirit, and ventured to make the truth audible.* Hence the improvised reply made by the Emperor to the deputation from the Legislative Body, on the 1st of January, 1814.†

On the 23rd of the same month, Sunday, the officers of the National Guard of Paris were ordered to assemble at the Tuileries in the Salle des Maréchaux. This salon is square, and very large ; it occupies the first floor of the Pavillon de l'Horloge. The officers, who were not informed of the purpose for which they were summoned, were about seven or eight hundred in number, and were all in uniform. They were ranged around the vast salon. At noon, Napoleon, who had crossed this apartment as usual on his way to the chapel, was saluted by repeated cries of "*Vive l'Empereur !*" On his return, he walked all round the room several times, and, after he had spoken to some of the chief officers, he placed himself in the centre.

* See Pièce Justificative, No. I., in Appendix.
† Idem., No. II.

Ten minutes afterwards, Marie-Louise entered the Salle des Maréchaux, accompanied by Madame de Montesquiou, who held the King of Rome in her arms. When she had taken her place by the Emperor's side, Napoleon addressed the National Guards, by whom he was surrounded, in a loud voice, to the following effect :—

"Gentlemen, a part of the territory of France is invaded ; I am about to place myself at the head of my army, and, with the help of God and the valour of my troops, I hope to drive the enemy back beyond the frontiers."

Then, taking the Empress and the King of Rome each by a hand, he added with emotion—

"If the enemy approaches the capital, I confide the Empress and the King of Rome—my wife and my son—to the devotion of the National Guard."

This simple address produced a great effect. Several of the officers stepped out of their ranks and kissed the Emperor's hands ; the greater number shed tears. Among the latter were many who were by no means partial to the imperial régime, but this scene had affected them.

After he had embraced his wife and his son for the last time, Napoleon left Paris on the 25th of January, 1814, at three o'clock in the morning, to place himself at the head of the small and hastily formed army, which formed his sole means of opposing the great host of soldiers from all the countries in Europe, now pouring down upon the north of France from every point. Each step that they took augmented their pretensions; but the Emperor still had the opportunity of making at least an honourable, if not a glorious, peace. Once more he held in his hands a treaty to which nothing but his signature was wanting. Most unhappily he achieved a partial success at that critical moment, and it stayed his hand. Once more he believed that the star which had guided him so long had reappeared above 'the horizon, and he declared that he would not think of peace until he had forced the enemy to re-cross the Rhine. Then it was that Napoleon executed the skilful movement which ought to have secured his triumph, but which in fact wrought his ruin. The enemy were to have found themselves enclosed in a square formed by all our divisions; the peasants, driven to despair by pillage and slaughter, were to have formed as many troops of light infantry, who should massacre the loiterers and the fugitives; but one of Napoleon's generals betrayed him, and gave passage to the Emperor of Russia and his army. The foreign troops were under the walls of the capital while Napoleon was confidently waiting to cut off their retreat.

I have heard distinguished generals say that his "Campaign of France" was his masterpiece of capacity, skill, and activity; that posterity, more just than his contemporaries, would place it in the first rank of the extraordinary things done by a man who had no equal ; and that, if he had been seconded, the enemy would have been destroyed, and Paris saved from their presence.

CHAPTER XIV.

THE UNCERTAINTY OF MARIE-LOUISE.

MARIE-LOUISE and her son were then at Paris, protected by the National Guard, to whom, as I have
already said, the Emperor had solemnly confided
them when he was going away. This corps showed
itself worthy of his confidence. The Empress had
intended to proceed to the Hôtel de Ville with the
King of Rome, but she was dissuaded from doing so.
Unfortunately she had about her only cowardly or
perfidious advisers, who combined together to hasten
her departure. She resisted for a long time, having
a great example for so doing in her own family—that
of Marie-Thérèse. What did she risk by remaining?

She was the daughter of one of the monarchs who had formed a confederacy against France; she was therefore certain of being treated with respect by the allied troops if they should enter Paris, and supposing Napoleon were to lose the crown, was it not possible that she might preserve it for his son? By leaving Paris, on the contrary, where the fate of France had always been decided for the last twenty-five years, she bade adieu to every hope, and left the field free to the partisans of the Bourbon dynasty, who now manifested their opinions openly. The confidence which the French had reposed in the invincibility of their army was already considerably weakened by the dangers which increased at every moment. The public plainly expressed a fear that the Allies would reach the gates of Paris, and several people had packed up their most precious goods in readiness to be despatched to the provinces farthest from the scene of war. At the same time, a great number of the inhabitants of the villages, farms, and country houses in the neighbourhood of the capital, came into Paris, bringing a more or less considerable portion of their furniture. The result was that the faubourgs, and all the roads leading to them, were encumbered with carts laden with goods, people of both sexes and all ages, and with cattle of every kind. The Empress had not a moment to lose, in gaining an open road by which to escape from the capital.

At last the Duke de Feltre succeeded in inducing her to leave Paris, by producing at the council a letter from the Emperor, in which he was instructed to send away the Empress and her son, if Paris was threatened. Napoleon added, "I would prefer to know that they were both at the bottom of the Seine, rather than in the hands of the foreigners." The Empress's departure was decided upon during the night of the 28th of March, and on the 29th, at eleven o'clock in the morning, the whole Court set out for Rambouillet, abandoning the capital to its fate.

A proclamation addressed to the Parisians had, however, been posted up, with a letter of King Joseph's as a sort of preface, but no measure of any kind for protection had been taken, not even the natural one of transferring the Senate and the Legislative Body to another city.

I cannot refrain from recording here an anecdote, which some will no doubt consider puerile, but which I regard as remarkable. When the moment of departure came, the little King of Rome, who was accustomed to make frequent excursions to St. Cloud, Compiègne, Fontainebleau, etc., would not leave his room. He screamed violently, rolled himself upon the ground, said that he would remain at Paris and that he would not go to Rambouillet. In vain did his governess promise him new toys; no sooner did she take him by the hand and try to lead him out, than he again flung himself down and struggled, screaming

K

still more loudly that he would not leave Paris. It was necessary to take him by force to a carriage.

I had remained in Paris to assist M. Ballouhai to collect several articles belonging to the Empress, which had been left behind in the haste of her departure. I was therefore at the Tuileries on the 1st of April (the day before the arrival of the Allies), when a general officer, the Prince of Wurtemberg, arrived. He asked us where the Empress was, and on learning that she had left Paris, he seemed greatly disturbed, and added that he had been charged to provide a guard for her, and to take the command of it. "What had she to fear?" said he to us. "The daughter of the Emperor of Austria was quite certain of our respect."

The drums had been beaten during a portion of the night of the 29th; all the National Guard was on foot—I will not say under arms, for a great portion of the men who composed it had only pikes. The chiefs had sent to the Duke de Feltre to ask for arms, and were told that he had none at his disposal; nevertheless when the Allied troops entered the capital, they found considerable stores of arms in the magazine.

From seven o'clock in the morning the firing of cannon was heard on every side.

The French army, which had quitted its position at Bondy, the day before, to fall back on Paris, was stopped at the heights of Montmartre and Belleville, already occupied by the army of observation under

command of Marshal de Ragusa. In accordance
with the plan made by the general council of the
Allies, the Prussian General, Blücher, was to attack
Montmartre, while the Russian corps, commanded by
General Barclay de Tolly, was to advance against
Belleville; but it was impossible for Blücher, who was
informed too late, to arrive in time to act in concert
with them, and on the 30th at seven o'clock in the
morning, such fierce fighting was going on between
Pantin and Romainville, that the position at Montmartre had not yet been threatened.

While the slaughter on the northern and eastern
heights was proceeding, Joseph Bonaparte was at Montmartre with his Staff. The sight of the danger seemed
to have roused a momentary energy in him, which he
seldom displayed. Fired by the example of the
brave soldiers by whom he was surrounded, he manifested confidence which did singular honour to French
valour, for he must indeed have entertained a lofty
idea of the bravery of the army, to persist in hoping
that he could yet defend besieged Paris, at the
moment when the enemy's troops entered the plain
of St. Denis. While he was occupied in giving orders
and making fresh dispositions of his troops, Colonel
Peyre, whom he had sent to reconnoitre, returned to
give an account of his mission. This superior officer
had been made prisoner by the Russians, and taken to
the Emperor Alexander; he was then able to estimate
the immense distance to which the forces of the enemy

extended. Being released by order of the Czar, he went at once to King Joseph, told him in detail all that he had seen, and assured him that resistance must be henceforth useless. Then Joseph, losing courage, exclaimed, "If that is the case, nothing remains but to parley."

But the brave soldiers who surrounded him, and who were enraged at the idea of yielding, cheered up his disconsolate mind, and, almost in spite of himself, he continued to give orders for fighting. Until then King Joseph had remained firm at his post; but when at length he saw that all hope was for ever lost for himself, his brother, and his family, forewarned by Marshal de Ragusa that his troops, harassed by a murderous fire, were about to be crushed by the overwhelming number of their assailants, and that it would then be impossible to preserve Paris from being occupied by main force, Napoleon's Lieutenant-General felt that the moment of his fall had arrived. He sent Colonel Peyre to Marshal de Ragusa with an authorization to demand a suspension of arms, and even a capitulation, if he judged it absolutely necessary. Having made these arrangements, Joseph abandoned Montmartre, re-entered Paris, and, two hours later, took the road to Blois in the hope of rejoining the Empress and the King of Rome, who had proceeded thither on the previous day.

On abandoning Montmartre, King Joseph left behind him only three hundred dragoons, commanded by an officer, to defend that important post. Twenty thousand men of the Silesian army, infantry and cavalry, then proudly advanced against this handful of heroes, who were animated equally by the love of their country and the love of glory. Far from trying to fly, they obstinately persisted in defending the post confided to them. They stood firmly by the guns which had protected them, and in the strength of their courage alone they charged the enemy with their accustomed impetuosity, and three times they had the triumph of repulsing that terrible mass of assailants. This would be an inconceivable thing had they not been Frenchmen. Three hundred Frenchmen to resist with some advantage twenty thousand foreigners! Nevertheless at every minute the ranks of these new Spartans were thinned, and soon, like those of Thermopylæ, they would all have perished, had not their commander, perceiving that they were about to be turned from the plain of Neuilly, ordered the retreat to be sounded, leaving the enemy amazed at the daring which had been displayed by all ranks of our army during the whole of this memorable day.

The artillery had been served on the Buttes de Chaumont by the pupils of the Polytechnic School— youths from seventeen to twenty years of age, who fought like old soldiers. The balls were exhausted, when a chest arrived. They opened it eagerly, and saw nothing in it but bread. They exclaimed, "We don't want bread, but balls." The balls were sent to them, but, either from treachery or in consequence of the confusion which prevailed, they were unserviceable, being too large for the guns.

During this time, the capital, abandoned to itself, had organized a Provisional Government, and capitulated with the Allied troops, who made their entry on the following day. Napoleon was almost a spectator of that entry, for he arrived on the same day, with one of his aides-de-camp, to reconnoitre the situation of the enemy. He was only five leagues away when he learned that Paris had capitulated; he then lost all hope, and returned to Fontainebleau utterly discouraged, as will be seen in the following chapter, which I have entitled, " Napoleon at Fontainebleau." Nevertheless he still had thirty thousand men of that Imperial Guard which was formerly so famous with him there. They loudly demanded that he should lead them to Paris, swearing to conquer or be buried under its ruins. The Emperor did not consent; although he had done everything in his power to deceive the inhabitants of the capital to the last moment, and to disguise from them the real state of things and their own situation; if at least we are to rely upon a bulletin written long beforehand, and which was to be printed in the *Moniteur* of the 31st. The original of this document was communicated in manuscript to me, and I have thought it sufficiently curious to give a copy of it here. For all this, however, Napoleon had done too much in favour of the city of Paris to be willing to destroy it. His refusal displeased the soldiers and cooled their enthusiasm.

The treachery of one of his generals, the reproaches of several others, the truths which the persons around him at length permitted themselves to speak, must have taught him then that flatterers are not friends. Lastly they pressed him to abdicate, and he made up his mind to that step.

The Empress merely passed through Rambouillet on her way to Blois, with the Council of Regency and a portion of the Guard.

On the 30th she slept at Chartres, on the 31st at Châteaudun, and on the 1st of April at Vendôme, where she arrived at three o'clock in the afternoon. The road from Vendôme to Blois was only in process of making, and the greater number of the vehicles, especially the most heavily laden, stuck in the mud. All the horses had to be used to extricate a few of them, and when these had been got out, the same operation was performed on the remainder. Thus was effected the flight of that Imperial Court which only a few days ago had been so brilliant !

At Blois the Court was in perfect security. The Allied troops had not yet advanced on that side, and Cristiani de Ravazan, Prefect of Loire-and-Eure, who had already been warned of the approach of Marie-Louise and her son, had proceeded to the boundary of his Department to " compliment " the Empress, when he received a communication from the Court which obliged him to return to Blois in all haste, and to evacuate the Hôtel de Ville in order to make it ready for the reception of the Court.

The principal inhabitants and functionaries, especially those residing near the prefecture, were requested to prepare lodging for Madame Mère; the Kings Joseph, Lucien, and Jérôme; the High Chancellor, Cambacères; the Ministers and Chiefs of Administration; and, finally, for eighteen hundred soldiers. On the 2nd of April, very early in the morning, the first detachment of cavalry began to arrive at Blois, and were speedily followed by immense quantities of baggage, and especially fifteen fourgons containing the treasury of the Imperial Court. The number of vehicles was so considerable, that the train of the Empress alone amounted to two hundred horses. These equipages, all huddled together, and covered with the mud they had collected during the journey, presented a singular appearance. It was the rain which cleaned them, for, in the existing state of things, the servants did not think proper to do anything of the kind. The superb State carriages, even that which had been used at the Emperor's marriage, were no better treated.

Couriers came in hour after hour. In the afternoon M. Cristiani de Ravazan set out to meet the Empress, a league from the city. The National Guard and the small garrison that remained placed themselves under arms, and at six o'clock a carriage in which the Empress and her son were seated appeared. It was followed by a great number of other carriages, containing her suite and all those persons who had accompanied her.   Her Imperial Majesty made her entry into Blois in the midst of a numerous crowd, who maintained unbroken silence.

Those Ministers who had gone so far as Tours, now began to arrive.   Several had remained at Orleans, others had fled to Brittany; of the latter number was Count Bigot de Préameneu, Minister of Public Worship, of whom I have already spoken, and Baron de Pomereul, Director-General of Publication.   They no doubt regarded the exercise of their peaceful functions as incompatible with the tumult of arms, and the aid of their counsels as superfluous.

For a few days after her arrival, Marie-Louise was left in ignorance of all that had taken place in Paris. The decisions of the Provisional Government and the decrees of the Senate were unknown to her: all the newspapers were kept from her; the Bourbons were never mentioned to her.   She therefore anticipated no other misfortune in addition to that of Napoleon's being obliged to make peace on any conditions that might be imposed upon him.

She was also far from imagining that the Emperor of Austria, her own father, meant to dethrone his son-in-law, and to deprive his grandson of a crown which he ought one day to wear.   It was not until the 7th of April, in the morning, that the truth was made known to her.

Madame D——, who had remained at Paris, was now to rejoin the Empress. On the 4th of April, certain persons came to her, and informed her that she would have to take important documents to Marie-Louise, which it was essential the Empress should receive without delay. Madame D—— procured a passport, obtained from General Sacken an order for an escort in case of need, left Paris on the 6th, and arrived at Blois on the 7th. She handed to her Majesty not only the papers which had been confided to her, but the decrees of the Provisional Government, and all the newspapers. The Empress had been kept in such complete ignorance of events, that she hardly believed what she read. The dispatches which Madame D—— had brought were from the small number of persons who remained faithful, and they urged and entreated her to return to Paris, before the arrival of a Prince of the House of Bourbon, assuring her of the Regency for herself and the throne for her son, if she would take this step. How easily it could be done was proved by the fact that the lady charged with these dispatches had travelled alone, in a post-chaise, with a single servant, and had not once had occasion to use her passport.

Marie-Louise promised to return to Paris; she seemed resolved to do so, on the very same evening, when Dr. Corvisart and Madame de Montebello opposed themselves to her project. The cowards composing the Council of Regency came to the support of these evil advisers. The unfortunate Princess was deceived anew, and she lost the opportunity of recovering what her flight had forfeited. A few days afterwards she learned simultaneously that Napoleon had abdicated, and that he had departed for the Isle of Elba. He was still permitted to be sovereign there.

CHAPTER XV.

NAPOLEON AT FONTAINEBLEAU.

THE EMPEROR LEAVES TROYES—HIS ARRIVAL AT THE "FONTAINE DE
JUVISY"—GENERAL BELLIARD—THE DUKE OF VICENZA—ARRIVAL AT
FONTAINEBLEAU—MARSHALS NEY AND MACDONALD—THE ABDICATION
OF NAPOLEON—MM. DÉJEAN AND DE MONTESQUIOU—ISABEY—THE
ALLIED COMMISSARIES—THE COURTYARD OF "LE CHEVAL BLANC"—
NAPOLEON'S WORDS—HIS DEPARTURE FROM FONTAINEBLEAU.

ON the 29th of March, 1814, at ten o'clock in the
morning, Napoleon left Troyes on horseback. He was
accompanied by General Bertrand, his Grand Marshal,
the Duke de Vicenza, his Grand Equerry, M. de
Saint Aignan, two aides-de-camp, and two orderly
officers. On the 30th, at two hours before daybreak,
the Emperor set out from Villeneuve for Vannes.
Since his departure from Troyes he had eaten nothing.
The ten first leagues had been travelled with the same
horses in less that two hours. He had not yet announced whither he was going, when at one o'clock
in the afternoon he arrived at Sens. After he had
rested there for a quarter of an hour, during which
time he drank half a cup of coffee without milk or
sugar, he left these gentlemen, whom, however, he

ordered to follow him, got into a wretched hack
carriage, accompanied by Bertrand only, and continued
his way towards the capital. Never was there
impatience equal to his ! He incessantly repeated,
" It will be too late, I shall not arrive." He changed
horses at Fromenteau, and arrived at half-past twelve
at the Cour de France, only five leagues from Paris,
such was the speed he had made.

Napoleon had hardly left his carriage, and seated
himself beside the Fontaine de Juvisy, while waiting
for fresh horses, when a convoy of artillery defiled
before him. It was the head of the first column of
troops, evacuating the capital after the affair that
had taken place in the morning. Then and there he
acquired the sad certainty that he had in fact arrived
twenty-four hours too late. Paris had just yielded to
the enemy, the Allies were to enter the next day (the
31st), at daybreak.

General Belliard, who accompanied his column,
announced the issue of the events of the day to the
Emperor, and he was soon placed in possession of the
terrible details of our great calamity.

Napoleon walked about on the road for nearly
twenty minutes without addressing a single word to
the generals of all arms, who followed one another
and hastened up to him. Presently he sent M. de
Caulaincourt to the head-quarters of the Allied Sovereigns ; then, entering the posting-house, he called for
a glass of water, which he drank without removing it

from his lips, and also for a map, which he studied for a long time. At four o'clock in the morning an express arrived from the Duke of Vicenza, who announced that all was over, that the capitulation had been signed two hours after midnight, and that Paris was for the moment under the protection of the National Guard. Napoleon got into his carriage, and immediately took the road to Fontainebleau. On his arrival there he shut himself up in his cabinet, and would not see any one.

On the 4th of April, the Emperor, having abdicated in favour of his son, nominated Marshals Ney, Macdonald, and Marmont to make known his resolution to the Allies. Marmont declined to accompany his colleagues into the presence of the Sovereigns. The proposal made in the name of Napoleon was rejected; the recall of the House of Bourbon had been decided upon. Without entering here into the details of the negotiations which took place between Napoleon and the Emperor Alexander, I shall content myself with saying that Marshals Ney and Macdonald, accompanied by the Duke of Vicenza, arrived from Paris on the 6th, between twelve and one o'clock in the morning. Marshal Ney told the Emperor that abdication pure and simple, without any addition beyond the guarantee of his personal safety, was exacted from him. Napoleon refused for some time to consent to this; finally he asked to what place he should be expected to retire.

"Sire, to the Isle of Elba," replied Ney, "with a pension of two millions a year."

"Two millions!" said Napoleon; "that is too much for me; since I am henceforth merely a soldier, one louis a day is quite enough for me."

Finally, the Act of Abdication * was signed at Fontainebleau, on the 11th of the same month.

During his stay at Fontainebleau, and after his abdication, the Emperor remained constantly in the library, reading or talking with the Duke of Bassano. He appeared several times in public as usual, for the purpose of reviewing his Grenadiers. During these last days a greater number of petitions than usual were presented to him, and, instead of giving them to an officer of his suite, he would put them in his coat pocket and read them in his cabinet. He often entered the gallery parallel with the library, and talked familiarly with any officers who were there, on the events of the day and on what the public papers said of him.

One day he came in with a newspaper in his hand,† and exclaimed indignantly, "They say that I am a coward!" In general he talked of political events as if he had no personal interest in them. He frequently spoke of Louis XVIII. "The French," said he, "will love him during the first six months,

* See "Pièce Justificative," No. 3.
† It was the *Gazette de France* of Monday, the 4th of April, 1814, No. 94.

they will grow cool about him during the next six months, and the following six, adieu! I know them!"

On reading an account of the harsh treatment that had been inflicted upon the Pope, he said, "That is true, the Pope was ill-treated, more ill-treated than I wished." Talking one morning with General Sebastiani, he observed that it was neither the Russians nor the other Powers that had conquered him, but liberal ideas, because he had oppressed them too much in Germany. Another time the Emperor sent for the Duke of Bassano, and, in the course of a conversation between them, these words were remarked: "You are reproached, Monsieur le Duc, with having constantly prevented me from making peace. What do you say to that?"

"Sire," replied the latter, "your Majesty knows very well I was never consulted, and your Majesty has always acted according to your own will, without taking counsel with the persons about you; I have not therefore found myself in a position to give you advice, but only to obey your orders."

"Ah! I know it well," replied the Emperor; "and what I say to you is only to let you know the opinion that is held of you."

Nevertheless, Napoleon appeared for some time to be occupied by a secret design. His mind was plainly dwelling upon the gloomiest passages of history. In his private conversations he dwelt incessantly upon the voluntary death which the men of antiquity did not hesitate to inflict upon themselves in such situations as this. His constantly and calmly discussing this subject created great uneasiness, and a circumstance occurred which added to the fears justly entertained by those around him.

The Empress had left Blois; she was anxious to rejoin her husband, and she had already arrived at Orleans; she was expected every moment at Fontainebleau, when all who were there learnt with astonishment, and from the mouth of the Emperor himself, that orders had been given to prevent her from carrying out her design.

During the night of the 12th–13th, at about one o'clock in the morning, the silence of the long corridors at Fontainebleau was suddenly broken by frequent comings and goings. The persons on duty in the château ascended and descended the stairs; candles were lighted in the apartments; everybody was on foot. One ran to knock at the door of Dr. Yvan, another to wake the Grand Marshal, a third to call the Duke of Vicenza, and a fourth to summon the Duke of Bassano, who was residing at the Chancellerie. All these personages arrived at the same time, and were taken into the Emperor's bedroom. In vain did astonishment, suspense, and curiosity lend an alarmed and attentive ear. Nothing could be heard but groans, and sobs, from the ante-chamber; the sounds reached the neighbouring gallery. All of a sudden Dr. Yvan

L

came out of the inner apartment, looking greatly agitated; he rushed down the grand staircase, wandered about for a minute in the court, found a horse tied to a railing, flung himself upon it and galloped off. The profoundest obscurity has always veiled the mysteries of that night.*

Isabey had made a water-colour portrait of the Empress Marie-Louise and her son, which she herself presented to the Emperor on the 1st of June, 1814. This portrait was now in the painter's possession.

* At the period of the retreat from Moscow, Napoleon had secured means to avoid falling alive into the hands of his enemies in case of accident. He had procured, through his surgeon Yvan, a sachet which he wore round his neck during the time that the danger lasted. Some said this was opium; others insisted that it was a preparation compounded by the celebrated Cabanis, and the same with which Condorcet the Deputy had destroyed himself;—whatever it was, Napoleon had preserved this sachet in one of the secret drawers of a travelling dressing-case which he always took on his campaigns. That night at Fontainebleau, he bethought him that the moment to have recourse to this terrible expedient had arrived. One of the valets, whose bed was placed behind his half-opened door, had heard him rise and seen him stir something into a coffee-cup, drink it, and lie down again. In a short time violent pains in the stomach and bowels forced from Napoleon the admission that he was dying. Then the man took upon himself to send for those who were most intimate with the Emperor. Yvan was not forgotten, and when he learned what had happened, and heard Napoleon complain that the action of the poison was not sufficiently rapid, he lost his head and rushed away from Fontainebleau. After a long swoon, followed by a profuse perspiration, the pains ceased, and the alarming symptoms disappeared, either because the dose had been insufficient, or because the poison had lost its strength through time. It is said that Napoleon, astonished to find himself still alive, reflected for a few moments, and then exclaimed, " God does not will it to be," and yielding himself into the hands of Providence, who had just saved his life, resigned himself to his new destinies.—Communicated note.

Having learned from M. de Caulaincourt that Napoleon
had expressed a desire to have it, Isabey hurriedly
set out for Fontainebleau, where he arrived on the
12th, at about noon. When he was ushered into
the Emperor's cabinet he found the Grand Marshal and
the Duke of Bassano there. On seeing him, Napoleon
cried, "Ah, it is Isabey! What news?" Isabey
answered that he had come to thank the Emperor for
all his kindness, and that, having learnt through the
Duke of Vicenza that he wished to have the portrait
of the Empress, he had brought it to him. Napoleon,
on receiving it, pressed his hand several times, without
saying one word. As the artist wore the uniform of
a Lieutenant of Grenadiers in the National Guard, the
Emperor said to him, "Isabey, are you also in the
National Guard?" He replied that although he had a
son in the army who had fought on the Plain of
Champagne, and of whose fate he was ignorant,* he
himself had never wished to return to Paris. Napoleon
added, "That is well, Isabey. Very well. I recognize
you there." The painter then retired.

Count Déjean, son of the ex-Minister of War, and
M. de Montesquiou, son of the Grand Chamberlain,
both generals of division, were sent to Paris by
Napoleon two or three days before his departure for
the Island of Elba. Count Déjean was so little able
to control himself and to conceal the profound grief

---

* Isabey learned, the next day, that his son had been killed in
battle, at Arcis-sur-Aube.

which the state of things occasioned him, that at
table he would come out of a dream when any one
addressed him, and he several times struck his fore-
head, muttering, " Is it possible ? Who could have
thought it ? Can it be ? " As for M. de Montesquiou,
he always answered with great precision and extreme
amenity.

On the 16th, the Commissaries who were to
accompany Napoleon, by his own desire, to the place
of embarkation, arrived at Fontainebleau.* They
were all received separately by the Emperor, who
said to Colonel Campbell, that " he had cordially
hated the English for fifteen years, but *he was at last
convinced that there was more generosity in their
Government than in that of the others.*"

The departure of the Emperor was to take place
on the 20th, at eight o'clock in the morning, and the
carriages were ready. The Imperial Guard was in
line in the great court of the Cheval Blanc, and an
immense crowd, composed of all the population of
Fontainebleau and the neighbouring villages, assembled
round the château. At eight o'clock in the morning,
however, the Commissaries having been introduced to
his apartment, found him still undressed and unshaved.
At eleven o'clock, General Bertrand having respectfully
observed to Napoleon that everything was ready for
his departure, the Emperor answered in an angry
tone. " And since when, Monsieur le Maréchal, have

* See " Pièce Justificative," No. 4.

I had to regulate my actions by your watch? I shall go away when it pleases me, and perhaps not at all."

Towards mid-day, the Emperor was in his cabinet with MM. de Flahaut and Ornano, when Bertrand announced to the Commissaries who were waiting in the ante-chamber, "His Majesty the Emperor." All ranged themselves on each side and in silence, according to the ordinary etiquette, which was observed up to the last moment; a door was opened, Napoleon appeared; he crossed the gallery rapidly, and descended the great staircase. So soon as he appeared in the court the drums beat. With an imposing wave of the hand he silenced them, and addressed the troops with so much dignity and warmth that all those who were present were profoundly touched. Then he clasped General Petit in his arms, kissed the Imperial Eagle, and said in a broken voice, "Adieu, my children! My best wishes will remain with you always. Preserve the remembrance of me." He gave his hand to be kissed by the officers who surrounded him. Napoleon's eyes were wet; all present wept. The emotion spread even to the Cossacks, although they did not understand a word of French. Several of his own servants who were to follow him burst into tears. The Emperor got into the carriage with General Bertrand; it was preceded by that of General Druot, and followed by the four carriages of the Commissaries. Eight others, with the Imperial arms, came after. They were occupied by the officers of the Imperial household. In a few minutes all these carriages disappeared, the Guard marched out of the château, and the crowd melted away in silence.

CHAPTER XVI.

THE chiefs of the Royalist party at Paris were not without anxiety respecting the resolution at which Marie-Louise might arrive, at Blois. Not only did they fear her return to the capital, but they did not wish her to follow her husband to the Island of Elba, because they dreaded that their reunion might sooner or later bring about a reconciliation between him and the Emperor of Austria. Prince Schwartzenburg was at their head. He was one of the firmest supporters of the party of the Emperor of Austria, and consequently he detested Napoleon and did not like Marie-Louise. Nevertheless, he kept on good terms with M. de Montesquiou and the few persons who possessed the confidence of Napoleon's wife. He gained over some, deceived others, and succeeded in making all aid in the execution of his projects.

So soon as the Empress was known to hesitate about what she should do, and that she talked of rejoining the Emperor at Fontainebleau, M. de Champagny was sent off to inform Prince Schwartzenburg, who was then in the neighbourhood of Troyes. The Prince despatched the Hetman of the Cossacks to Blois on the spot, and he arrived at the moment of the Empress's departure for Orleans. The troops by whom he was accompanied formed the vanguard. They pillaged a fourgon containing bonnets and caps, they would probably have pillaged all the carriages, if their chief had not appeared on the spot and made them restore the spoil.

When the Emperor's brothers Joseph and Jérôme were apprised of the abdication of Napoleon, they strenuously endeavoured to induce Marie-Louise to repair to Tours with them and the army which was to cross the Loire. Their entreaties were urgent, but they did not transgress the respect which they owed to their sister-in-law. I was in the adjoining room. The Empress, who had made up her mind to go to Orleans, refused to accompany them. They left her and departed from Blois. The narrative of M. de Bausset is a fable.

During this time the perfidious advisers of the unfortunate Empress employed all their skill to dissuade her from rejoining her husband. It was represented to her, on the one side, that the climate of the Island of Elba would be fatal to her health, and, on the other, that Napoleon, whose fall from his throne was partly due to the arms of his father-in-law, and who was reduced to a petty sovereignty, would no longer regard her as he did in the past, and that she would have to bear his incessant reproaches. It was added that, in the interest of her son, she ought to rejoin her father, who had always loved her, and would certainly secure a principality for her preferable to the Island of Elba ; and that she might even induce him to take some step favourable to Napoleon. One only among her ladies ventured to tell her that her duty and her honour demanded that she should follow her husband into his exile.

"You are the only one who hold this language to me," said the Empress; "all my friends, and, above all, Madame de C——, advise me to the contrary."

"Madame," replied the lady who had given her this advice, "that is because I am the only one who does not deceive your Majesty." *

Marie-Louise preferred, however, to follow the counsel of those whom she ought to have mistrusted, all the more readily that they began to let out their true feelings. "Oh, how I wish that all this was over and done with !" said Madame de Montebello,

---

* After Marie-Louise had seen her father at Rambouillet, she expressed to Madame D—— her bitter regret that she had not followed her advice.

while breakfasting with her on the very day when they were to set out for Orleans; "how I should like to be quiet, with my children, at my little house in the Rue d'Enfer!" "What you say, Madame la Duchesse, is very hard," replied the Empress, with tears in her eyes, but she reproached her no further. The Lady-in-Waiting had already formally declared, that in no case whatever would she go to the Island of Elba. It is therefore reasonable to suppose that, if she had really entered into the plot to separate Marie-Louise from Napoleon, it was because she wanted to avoid either the disgrace of refusing to follow the Empress or the sacrifice of her inclination by accompanying her.

She did, however, attend her so far as Vienna.

On her arrival at Orleans, the Empress found there several regiments who were greatly exasperated, and raised by day and night, but especially by night, cries of "Vive l'Empereur!" The Commissaries of the Government arrived at the municipality, bringing orders from the new rulers, and the white cockade. The inhabitants, although very Royalist, dared not assume this, so much afraid were they of exciting the anger of the soldiery.

It was proposed to the Empress that she should profit by the sentiments of the garrison who surrounded her, to rejoin her husband. She pleaded the dangers of the road. She was assured that there were no dangers—and that was quite true. But Madame de

M—— and Madame D—— stood alone in their advice against the persons to whom the Empress was most attached. Another method proposed by them was equally rejected. In vain did they use the most respectful solicitations. Marie-Louise was quite willing to rejoin Napoleon, but being assailed by so many different opinions, and unable to distinguish rightly between their respective sincerity, she was so unfortunate as to follow the advice of those who desired to replace her in her father's hands, and to separate her from Napoleon. This they succeeded in doing. During her short stay at Orleans, M. Dudon came, in execution of the Articles of Abdication by the Emperor, as Commissary of the Provisional Government, to demand the crown jewels, the treasure, the plate, etc.

Each time that a "Journey of Representation" was made by the Court, the crown jewels and all ornaments which the Empress would require were given in charge to one of the ladies of the household. The individual receiving them gave a receipt, which was returned to her when she restored the jewels. Just before the departure of the Empress the usual receipt was given to M. de la Bouillerie, who sent M. Dudon to Orleans, to take away all the precious objects "belonging to the Crown."

A dispute then arose between M. Dudon and the lady who had the jewels in charge during the journey. The latter claimed an "esclavage" of pearls which the Empress had on her neck at the time. This neck-

lace, composed of a single row of pearls, had cost
500,000 livres, and had been given by the Emperor
to the Empress shortly after the birth of her son.
It had always made a portion of her private jewellery.
M. de la Bouillerie had never claimed it, but M. Dudon
now did so. A lady of the household went to the
Empress, who was in her salon, surrounded by a
numerous company, and informed her of the dispute.
At the first word, Marie-Louise unclasped the neck-
lace, and putting it into the lady's hands said : " Give
it to him and make no remark."

When Bonaparte was made First Consul, there were
no crown jewels remaining except the " Regent,"
which was then in pawn at Berlin for four millions.
He redeemed it, and acquired or obtained by his
victories jewels which now constitute those of
the Crown of France, and are of great value. By
the Emperor's orders we delivered them all up to the
Commissary of the Provisional Government who had
come to claim them in the name of M. de la Bouillerie.
He also received the magnificent table services, the
Coronation service in vermeil, which was a masterpiece of workmanship, and an immense quantity of
plate. The whole was placed in twenty-one fourgons.
The twenty-second contained thirty-two little barrels
each enclosing a million in gold. This fourgon, which
was placed in the Court of the Secrétariat, at the
Episcopal Palace, was seen by all the National Guards
who lined the first court at the moment when, in the

name of the Emperor, the thirty-two little barrels were handed over to M. Dudon, the Government Commissiary. These twenty-two fourgons started for Paris, whither I went the following day. I found them at Étampes, where I counted them anew.

When the fourgon laden with gold arrived at the Tuileries, the Count d'Artois, who was there with his suite, ordered four barrels to be brought to him. He had them opened, and said to all who were present: "Help yourselves, gentlemen; we have suffered together, we ought to share the present good fortune." Each took as much as he could carry, and the barrels were soon empty. I have this anecdote from an officer of the National Guard who was on duty in the apartment and witnessed the distribution. I have thought it right to dwell upon the handing over of the treasure at Orleans, at which myself and several persons were present, in order to refute a lying assertion contained in the newspapers of the time, which affirmed that the Princes Joseph and Jérôme had pillaged the treasure. I have given an account of the facts. It is asserted that none of the gold was ever restored to the Treasury; others say that twenty millions were restored. I am entirely ignorant of the truth in this respect.

On the 3rd of April, Palm Sunday, Mass was said at the palace by M. Gallais, Curé of the Church of St. Louis, for there was neither almoner, chaplain, nor clerk of the Imperial Chapel among the persons in the

suite of the Empress.   After Mass, a council was held
by the Ministers.   At five o'clock, her Majesty received
the authorities of the city, without any address on
their part on account of the circumstances.   Marie-
Louise, followed by her son, passed through the ranks
of these authorities, addressing a few words to each of
them, beginning with the clergy—a remarkable inno-
vation, which did honour to the piety of the Empress.
The most profound sadness was depicted on her
face.   She dined alone, and did not receive any one
afterwards.

The next day, at three o'clock in the afternoon,
the Kings Joseph and Jérôme, accompanied by the
Minister of War, left Blois for Orleans.   I have heard
it said that the object of their journey was to ascertain
whether it would not be well to establish the Regency
in that city, in order to render communication with
the Emperor more easy; but on their arrival at Orleans
at three o'clock in the morning, the two Kings received
despatches from Fontainebleau, in which Napoleon's
displeasure with the Regency was expressed in terms
of the most violent anger.   Without doubt the
Emperor attributed the capitulation of Paris to the
flight of Joseph, whom he had nominated Lieutenant-
General of the Empire, and to whom he had sent orders
to remain at his post.

It was only there that they became aware of
Napoleon's order of the day, dated 4th April, 1814.*

* See "Pièce Justicative," No. 5.

The fact is, that the two brothers returned to Blois on the following morning.

On Wednesday, the 6th, the pupils of the Polytechnic School, and the schools of St. Cyr and Châlons, with the pages and the greater part of the civil household of the Emperor, arrived. The carriages, now become useless, were sent to Tours, the Coronation carriage was despatched to Chambord. The city of Blois was full; there was not an inhabitant who had not shared his house, his room, or even his bed with the newly arrived guests. Then did Blois offer a striking picture of the instability of human things. During the stay of the Empress at Blois and at Orleans, a daily correspondence had been established between herself and Napoleon, who was expecting her arrival. She wrote to him that it was her intention to have an interview with her father, and to implore his support for her husband. This plan not having obtained his approbation, she had him informed that her health required that she should "take the waters," and she asked his consent to her making the journey. Napoleon, perceiving that the intention was to separate him from his wife, sent off a numerous detachment of his Guard on the moment, and followed it closely; but notice was given of his departure, and that of the Empress was hurried on. On arriving at Étampes he learnt that Marie-Louise had already passed through that town on her way to Rambouillet, where she remained several days, awaiting her father.

At Rambouillet she received a visit from the Emperor of Russia, who wished to see "the little King" (by this title he asked for him). The King of Prussia came afterwards, and he, too, wished to see "the little King." Finally the Emperor of Austria arrived. The interview was affecting; he wept with his daughter and embraced his grandson; nevertheless, both one and the other were ruthlessly sacrificed.

Napoleon, having arrived too late at Étampes (the Empress having passed through an hour before), could not attempt to follow her, since the whole country was occupied by the Allied troops. He returned to Fontainebleau, entertaining no doubt of his wife's feelings, and convinced that she had been forced to withdraw herself. Knowing nothing of the intrigues by which she was surrounded, he found it difficult to believe in the ingratitude of most of those whom he had laden with favours, several of whom did not even wait for his departure to throw off the mask and reveal the reality. His commissaries and his generals never left off reminding him of the advice that they had given him on such and such occasions, and declared that, if it had been followed, matters would have turned out differently. In fact, he was the sick lion in the fable, whom all the animals came to insult in their turn, neither was the kick of the ass spared him.

A despicable Mameluke, whom he had brought back from Egypt and attached to his private service, on whom he had already settled four or five thousand livres annually, insisted upon being paid forty thousand francs to go with him, and, after having received the money, he left Paris and returned no more. Constant, his first valet-de-chambre, also exacted a sum of forty thousand francs to go with him to the Island of Elba, and, after having received it, disappeared from Fontainebleau the very day before the Emperor's departure.

Of all the persons attached to the personal service of Napoleon, MM. Hubert and Paillard, whom the Emperor had not named to accompany him,—quite young men, highly educated, and bound to their country by domestic ties,—were the two who replaced the fugitives, and in their fidelity there was no mercenary motive. They did not return to France until they had placed M. Marchand, whose fidelity to the Emperor is so well known, in a position to act as their substitute. M. Colin, the Emperor's maître d'hôtel, gave his master a similar proof of attachment, and did not quit the Island of Elba until the state of his health forced him to return to France.

On leaving Paris, the high functionaries of the Imperial Court, as well as the great dignitaries of the Crown, had had no time to provide themselves with passports, nor, indeed, had they thought of doing so, relying upon their titles for security; but that which had been a safeguard when they were leaving the capital, became a danger when they were leaving Blois. They were obliged to pass through a long

M

line of Allied troops, and the rank of a minister or
favourite of Napoleon, far from being a title of recommendation, became on the contrary a motive for persecution. This new state of affairs was discussed, and
it was resolved that passports should be procured from
the Mayor of Blois, and M. de Schouvaloff be requested
to affix his *visa* to them.

The first of these requests was attended with no
difficulty, except in its execution, which was unpleasant
because a personal description of each " Excellency "
was indispensable. But the head clerk of the Mairie, M.
Bruère, acquitted himself of his task with all the tact
and consideration demanded by the singular position
of these great personages. The worthy functionary
would have wished to escape this necessity, and it was
not without sharing their own feelings, that he set
down in writing, the features of kings, princes,
ministers, great officers of State, and other individuals,
who taxed his zeal without exhausting it, notwithstanding that he had to fill up four hundred passports.*

This, however, was only the first of two operations :
the second concerned Count Schouvaloff. A few hours
after the Austrian General had arrived at the head-
quarters of the Allied Sovereigns, the chiefs of the
Paris Government presented themselves with their

---

* These four hundred passports produced a profit of eight hundred
francs—the only revenue that the city of Blois derived from the
accidental sojourn of the Imperial Government.—Communicated note.

passports, to receive his *visa*. Very soon the room in the Hôtel de la Galère, where he was lodged, was found too small to contain the number of applicants, each of whom wanted his own special business done quickly and done first. Those who had procured letters of recommendation arrived with their letters, and presented them to the General; who replied, on receiving them, that he had the highest consideration for their writers, but that, so great was the pressure on his time, he was obliged to beg each applicant either to wait or to return. Nevertheless, his treatment of the different functionaries made it evident that he was aware of the conduct of each of them. It was remarked that he lent himself to everything that could be agreeable to the Duke de Feltre, and that he did not sign the passport of the Duke of Rovigo until after he had written on the margin, " M. de Savary."

While Napoleon and most of the members of his family and of his Government were quitting France (that France which the Emperor had rendered so great and so powerful), Marie-Louise was leaving the country in another direction. On her departure from Rambouillet * she was obliged to stop at Gros

---

* When she left Rambouillet she was accompanied by her son and by Madame de Montesquiou, governess to the young Prince, and attended by Madame Soufflot, the under-governess, and also by Madame Marchand, first " berceuse," and mother of M. Marchand, whose devotion to the Emperor is so well known. She was rejoined at Gros Bois by the Duchess of Montebello and Madame Corvisart, who accompanied her to Vienna.

Bois, where she remained for two days, being indisposed. She returned to Vienna by the southern route, and passed through the Tyrol, where she was forced to be present at several fêtes. For these she had little heart; but such were the orders of Francis II.

At last she arrived at Vienna, but she had brought a numerous and brilliant suite, and this displeased her stepmother, again exciting her jealousy. She was sent away to Schönbrunn, where she was visited tolerably frequently by her sisters, but very rarely by her father and the Empress.*

It was at this time that Madame (the Duchesse d'Angoulême) wrote to the Empress of Austria, saying that, if Marie-Louise had left in Paris any persons in whom she took an interest, she, the Duchess, would undertake to protect them, and procure them employment. This generous offer was communicated by the Empress to her step-daughter, who accepted it, and sent a list of the names of four individuals—one woman, and three men. I do not know what her Royal Highness has done in favour of these latter,

* Everybody knows that the Dauphiness was the aunt, "à la mode de Bretagne," of Marie-Louise. Queen Marie Antoinette was the sister of Caroline Queen of Naples. Madame d'Orleans, the Empress of Austria (mother of Marie-Louise), and the Prince who was the father of the Duchesse de Berri, were all three children of Queen Caroline, and consequently, all three, cousins to Madame d'Angoulême. The Empress Marie-Louise, the Duke de Berri, and the children of the Duchess of Orleans are all nephews and nieces of the Dauphiness, "à la mode de Bretagne;" and the Duke de Bordeaux (the late Count de Chambord), as well as the son of Marie-Louise (the deceased Duke de Reichstadt), were her grand-nephews in the same manner.

but I had the good fortune to be the woman recommended to the kindness of the august Princess, and I have obtained a pension for the former services of my husband, and a *bourse* for my son at the College of Henry IV. I shall preserve a grateful memory of these favours all my life.

Marie-Louise, on her return to Vienna, found there her grandmother Caroline, ex-Queen of Naples, who blamed her severely for having deserted her husband. Marie-Louise excused herself on the plea of the obstacles that had been raised to her reunion with him. " My daughter," said the ex-Queen, " one can always jump out of a window. What will the world say of you ? It will judge you severely." Marie-Louise, who lacked strength of character, and had no confidence in herself, could not be reconciled to the unfortunate circumstances in which she was placed. She was surrounded at Vienna and at Parma by persons devoted to the Empress of Austria and to M. de Metternich. The enmity of the Austrian Cabinet to Napoleon was not satisfied. He had still to be wounded through all he held most dear, and nothing was omitted that could intensify his misfortunes.

It was represented to Marie-Louise that divorce was necessary, that circumstances absolutely imposed it upon her, and those persons in whom she had the greatest confidence were employed to use all their influence to induce her to consent. Count de Bausset, who was at the head of her household, and Madame

de Brignolet, who had been appointed Lady-in-Waiting
after the departure of the Duchess of Montebello
(she had remained only two days at Vienna, and had
left that city with Corvisart), employed every means
of persuasion during several months to bring the
Empress to the point of making this sacrifice. They
never succeeded. Having fallen ill some time afterwards, Madame de Brignolet acknowledged on her
deathbed the harm which she had done, and implored
forgiveness from Marie-Louise. This she easily
obtained. She also made the same request to Madame
de Montesquiou, to whom she had done all sorts of
ill offices, not only with Marie-Louise, but also with
the Empress of Austria. Let me say here, that every
effort in the direction of divorce proved useless.
Napoleon's wife declared bravely that she chose to
retain that title, and that she would never give her
consent to any proceedings tending to a divorce.

Such was the state of things in Austria, when
Napoleon quitted the Island of Elba. On the 12th of
April, Madame Mère left Blois with Cardinal Fesch,
her brother, who had arrived there only the evening
before, by a long and winding road. After the first
alarm, which had been given at Lyons on the 12th of
January, his Eminence found himself in a difficulty
between his family affections and his love for his
country. The voice of kindred, however, being the
stronger, prevailed with the Cardinal. He left his
See, and followed the civil authorities to Roanne, but

ill pleased by the spirit of the Lyonnese, who, he said, "had been so stupid as not to defend themselves," he went from Roanne to Pradines, and took up his abode in a religious house which he had founded; but he was soon obliged to abandon this retreat, where he narrowly escaped being taken by a detachment of the Allies' cavalry, passing through by chance. He had barely time to mount a horse and escape. His apartment was visited as an object of curiosity, but there was no violation of the rights of property. His stables were also visited, but not equally respected. The troopers found some fine remount horses there, and considered themselves free to dispose of them in the absence of their owner. From Pradines his Eminence reached Auvergne, then Lower Languedoc, and finally the banks of the Loire, arriving at Blois just in time to leave the city. The Cardinal arrived at Orleans on Easter Sunday, and set out for Rome on the following day, taking with him Madame Mère.

The Kings Jérôme and Joseph were lost in the crowd. Louis had remained at Blois, where some interest in him was shown. He also found a more solid source of consolation in religion, and on Palm Sunday and Good Friday he attended Mass in the parish church of St. Louis, wearing the uniform of a General of Division. Soon afterwards he went to Switzerland, with the intention of settling on an estate which he possessed in the neighbourhood of Lausanne, and living there as a private gentleman.

Jérôme and Joseph passed eight days in Orleans and its neighbourhood, and departed on the 18th, also taking the road to Switzerland. I was told that Jérôme remained several days at La Motte Beuvron, where he distributed money to the troops passing through, in order to rally them to the cause of his brother Napoleon.

CHAPTER XVII.

ON leaving Fontainebleau, Napoleon was received
everywhere with cries of "Vive l'Empereur!" and
the foreign Commissaries had much to suffer from
the insults heaped on them by the people all along
the road. On the following day, most of the journals
of the capital endeavoured, by weak witticisms, to
lessen the effect produced by the grand scene which
had preceded his departure. But all who were not
entirely devoid of generosity, whether friends or
enemies, were affected by it. The foreign Commissaries who were witnesses of that scene, moved by an
involuntary impulse of enthusiasm, had waved their
hats in the air, and when she heard the account of it,
Madame de Staël herself was thrilled with emotion.*

* For details of this scene the reader may be referred to the en-
graving of M. Horace Vernet, " Les Adieux à Fontainebleau." The

It is an undeniable fact that the soldiers who were present wept profusely while Napoleon was speaking, and that some officers broke their swords on re-entering the city.

The Emperor said several remarkable things in conversation during this sad journey. I shall only quote here those which I have received from oral witnesses, because they alone are worthy of attention. He knew that he had been bitterly reproached with not having inflicted death upon himself. "I see nothing great," said he, "in ending one's life as if one had been dishonoured, or had lost one's fortune at play. There is much more courage in surviving a great and unmerited misfortune. I have never feared death. This I have proved in more than one fight, and very lately at Arcis-sur-Aube."*

"I have nothing with which to reproach myself. . . . I have not been an usurper, *as they persisted in saying everywhere*. I accepted the crown only by the unanimous desire of the nation. . . . As for the wars that I have made, that is another thing. I believed it my duty to make them, since France required to be extended." He afterwards said to General Köller, "Well, General, you heard me speak to my old Guard

fidelity of the portraits and the exactness of the attitudes render this composition a valuable historical monument.

* Before leaving Arcis, and after the fight, Napoleon sent two thousand francs, by Count de Turenne, from his private purse, to the Sisters of Charity, in order that they might have the means of relieving the needs of the wounded and the poor.

yesterday; you saw the effect I produced. That is the way to speak and act with them, and if Louis XVIII. does not follow this example, he will never make anything of the French soldier."

These words led him to praise the Emperor Alexander, for the amicable and generous manner in which he had treated Louis XVIII. and most of the Princes of his family, when he went to ask for an asylum in Russia. "That," added he, "is treatment which I should vainly have expected from my father-in-law; nevertheless, I had some rights, it seems to me."

That day he kept Colonel Campbell to dinner, and talked much to him of the last campaign. "But for that animal L——," said he, "who made me believe that it was Schwartzenburg who was pressing me at St. Dizier, while it was only Wintzingerode, and but for that other brute D——, who was afterwards the cause of my descending upon Troyes, where I counted upon disposing of four thousand Austrians and did not find a cat, I should have marched to Paris, arrived there at the same time as the Allies, and not been to-day where I am." Then, after a long pause, he added, "But I have always been ill surrounded. And then those rogues of prefects! that M——, that T——, who assured me that the levies of troops were going on with the greatest success; and that traitor M——, who finished the business. But there are also other marshals equally ill-intentioned, among others S——, whom indeed I have always known, both him and his wife, to be schemers. She was the constant cause of my quarrels with that poor Josephine."

He talked for a long time of the ill conduct of the Senate towards him. M. and Madame Guizot, who were coming back from the south, saw him at Tarare, while he was changing horses. He spoke to the persons standing around his carriage, as a sovereign, and asked them, among other things, whether they had suffered much in the last war. These all answered him by the unanimous cry of "Vive l'Empereur!" At Salvagny, the last post before Lyons, he stopped for supper. Having finished, Napoleon left his Commissaries and walked alone up the road. He met the Curé, accosted him, and asked him whether the inhabitants of his Commune appeared satisfied with the change of Government. Then, pointing to the sky where the stars were shining, he added, that he had once known the names of all those constellations, but had since forgotten them, and begged the Curé to tell him how one, to which he pointed with his hand, and which seemed brighter than the others, was named. The good Curé having replied that he knew nothing about it, the Emperor bowed to him, smiling, and returned to the inn.

The Emperor passed Lyons on the 23rd, at eleven in the evening. Some groups who assembled round his carriage, raised the cry of "Vive Napoleon!" of which he took no notice. The next day, towards noon, he met Marshal Augereau near Valence.

Napoleon and the Marshal got out of their carriages at the same time. The Emperor held out his arms to Augereau, and they embraced each other.

"Where are you coming from?" said Napoleon to the Marshal, taking his arm familiarly, and using the familiar "tutoiement." "Are you going to Court?" Augereau replied that he was only going to Lyons; and they walked along the road to Valence for a quarter of an hour. I know from an authentic source the result of this interview. Napoleon affectionately reproached the Marshal for his conduct towards him, and said in conclusion, " Your proclamation is very stupid. Why do you abuse me?—you! my old companion! You should simply have said, 'The will of the nation has been pronounced in favour of the new Sovereign; the duty of the army is to conform to it. Vive le Roi!'" *

Augereau then began to make some strong remarks upon his ambition, and his obstinacy in never listening to the advice of anybody, declaring that to this obstinacy he had sacrificed everything—his companions in arms, his fortunes, and even the welfare of France. Napoleon, tired of all this, turned away rudely; then, coming back to the Marshal, he pressed his hand, and said, " Adieu, Augereau. I am astonished that it should be you who thus reproach me. Come, however, embrace me again." Then he flung himself into his carriage. Augereau, with his hands behind

* See " Pièce Justificative," No. 7.

his back, stayed for some time in the same place, without even removing the forage-cap which he wore. The Emperor drove off, and, turning back in the carriage, waved him a last farewell with his hand. The Marshal resumed his seat in his carriage after having saluted the Commissaries.

At a short distance from Avignon he changed horses, and found several people assembled to see him pass by. He was received with cries of "Vive le Roi! Vivent les Alliés! À bas Nicolat! À bas le tyran! À bas le gueux," etc. This multitude, pursuing him with foul invectives, ran after his carriage and clung to it, endeavouring to see him so as to insult him more grossly. The Emperor was to some extent hidden from them by Bertrand, who stood up at one of the windows. He did not say a word.

Having reached Saint-Canat, he stopped at a miserable inn called La Calade, situated on the highroad. He sat down to table with Bertrand without uttering a word, and, as he was unknown to the hostess, who thought they were merely members of the suite accompanying him, he entered into conversation with her. "Well," said the woman to him, "what about Bonaparte now? What does he say? Is it long since you left him?"

"No," replied the Emperor.

"I am curious to see whether he will succeed in escaping," said she. "I am afraid the people want to massacre him, but we must acknowledge that he deserves it, the villain. But do tell me, are they going to embark him for his island ? "

" I believe so."

"They will drown them, won't they ? "

" I hope so."

The hostess having gone out, Napoleon turned to Bertrand, and took his arm. "You see, my friend," said he, "to what dangers I am exposed—and you !"

Bertrand replied only by tears, which he endeavoured to hide with his two hands.

At Saint-Maximin, the Emperor breakfasted with the Commissaries who accompanied him. Hearing it said that the Sub-Prefect of Aix was in the place, he sent for him, and addressed him in these terms—

" I came into the midst of you with perfect confidence, and I find here only madmen, who are threatening my life. It seems to me that these Provençaux are a foul race ; they committed all sorts of horrors and crimes in the Revolution, and they seem disposed to begin again. But when it is a question of fighting bravely, then they are—cowards ! Never did Provence furnish me with a single regiment upon which I could count. Can you not restrain this populace ? "

The Sub-Prefect not knowing how to answer, or whether he ought to excuse himself before the foreign Commissaries, merely said, " I am quite confused, Sire."

Napoleon then asked him whether the " droits réunis " were already abolished, and whether a " levée en masse " would have been difficult to effect.

"A 'levée en masse,' Sire !" replied the Sub-Prefect. "I have never been able to get together half of the contingent which ought to be annually furnished for the conscription."

Napoleon again expressed himself strongly respecting the Provençaux, and then dismissed the Sub-Prefect.

He afterwards related, that, eighteen years before, he had been sent into this province with several thousand men, to deliver some Royalists who were to have been hung for having worn the white cockade. "I saved them with a great deal of difficulty from the hands of these ruffians," said he, "and now they would perpetrate the very same outrages against any man among them who should not wear that very same cockade ! Ah !—they are true Frenchmen !"

The following day they were to have arrived at Fréjus. The escort's carriage, preceding that of the Emperor, reached the house of M. Charles, a former legislator, after dinner. His country seat is situated near the lake, and Princess Pauline Borghese, Napoleon's sister, had been staying there some months on account of her delicate health. She shuddered at the narrative of the dangers which her brother had incurred during his journey, which was given her by the Commissaries; and from that moment she resolved to accompany him to the Island of Elba, and never more to leave him. It was with great difficulty that she could be made to believe in the events which had just taken place, and when at last it was impossible for her to refuse the evidence of their authenticity, she exclaimed, " If this be so, my brother is dead." They then assured her that the Emperor was well, that a handsome allowance was secured to him, and that he was on the way to his new destination. " How," said she, "has he been able to bear up under all this?" She then fainted, and when she came to herself was much more ill than before. The interview which she had on that same day with her brother, still further injured her health. She started in the evening for Muy, so that she might have only two leagues to travel on the morrow.

When the Emperor arrived at Fréjus, some of the individuals who at Fontainebleau had seemed willing to partake his exile in the Island of Elba, forsook him. It was probably one of these persons who thought proper to appropriate the cash-box of his maître d'hôtel, whose business it was to defray the expenses of the journey, and who still had nearly sixty thousand francs in his possession. This robbery was committed during the night, on the 26th–27th.

Colonel Campbell was at Fréjus, having arrived at Marseilles with an English frigate, the *Undaunted*. This vessel was commanded by Captain Asher, and was to escort the Emperor, in order to secure his ship from every sort of attack. According to the treaty, Napoleon was to have been taken to Elba in a corvette, and he was very much displeased to find only the brig

N

L'Inconstant, which was to receive its dethroned sovereign and remain in his possession. After a moment's hesitation he preferred the English frigate, not choosing it to be said that he had been exiled under the French flag.

That day the Emperor invited to dinner, not only all the Commissaries, but also the Captain of the English vessel. During dinner he complained to General Köller of the injustice of every sort with which he had been treated; that he had been left only a shabby table-service in silver, and six dozens of shirts; that all the rest of his linen and plate had been retained, as well as a quantity of things which he had bought with his own money. He was particularly indignant that his exclusive right to the " Regent," which he had redeemed from Berlin at a cost of four millions, had not been recognized. The great diamonds had, in fact, been placed in pawn by the French Government, for eight hundred thousand crowns, with the Berlin Jews. He begged the General to carry his complaint to his Emperor, and to the Emperor of Russia, hoping that by the aid of those Sovereigns justice would be done to him.

On the morning of the 28th, Napoleon would have wished to embark with his suite, but he was not well, and he could not depart until nine o'clock in the evening. General Schouvaloff went on board the frigate as if the Emperor were there already. He was charged for the last time to present his homage to the Emperor Alexander.

Austrian Hussars had accompanied him to Port Saint-Raphau, where he had landed fourteen years before on his return from Egypt. He was received with military honours and a salute of twenty-four guns. Two hours afterwards the frigate sailed. All the Commissaries accompanied the Emperor to the Island of Elba.

His suite was composed of Generals Bertrand and Druot, the Polish Major Germanofsky, the paymaster, M. Peyroche; a doctor, M. Fourrau; two equerries; his maître d'hôtel, M. de Caulaincourt; one valet-de-chambre, M. Hubert; two cooks and six domestics, coachman, footman, and grooms.

The Emperor was calm. General Bertrand could not conceal his emotion. General Druot maintained his courage and cheerfulness throughout these melancholy circumstances. I was assured that Napoleon wished to give him a hundred thousand francs, but he distinctly refused to accept the present, saying, "Sire, if I accepted your money, my sincere affection to your Majesty would be attributed to interested motives. Keep it, however; we never know what may happen."

CHAPTER XVIII.

ON the 3rd of May, 1814, at daybreak, the *Un-daunted* sighted the Island of Elba.   General Druot and Colonel Klamm were sent ashore, the former in his capacity as the Emperor's Commissary, the second as charged by the French Government to require General Dalesmes, Governor of the island, to resign his command to General Druot, Napoleon's Pleni-potentiary.

The two Deputies found the inhabitants of Elba in a state of complete anarchy.   At Porto-Ferrajo the white flag was flying, at Porto-Longone the tri-colour. The rest of the island wished to proclaim its indepen-dence.   When the news of the arrival of Napoleon was spread, and especially that of the treasure he was bringing with him, all parties united, and went to meet their new Sovereign.   General Druot received the keys of the city from the Governor. All the stores, the munitions of war, the fort and its artillery were handed over to him without any difficulty. After this the new Imperial flag was hoisted on the tower of Porto-Ferrajo, and Colonel Klamm returned on board to report the issue of his mission to the Emperor.*

At noon Napoleon set foot on shore,† and General Druot saluted him with one hundred guns fired from the forts. The Municipality and the State bodies, came to receive and address him. Napoleon replied, " The mildness of your climate, the proximity of your island to France, have led me to choose it for my abode. I hope you will rightly appreciate this preference, and that you will love me like dutiful children. You will always find me disposed to extend to you the solicitude of a father and of a good sovereign."

The Emperor was conducted to the Hôtel de Ville, where he was to be lodged provisionally. The great hall, which served for public meetings and balls, had been ornamented with some pictures and crystal candelabra; a sort of throne had been erected, and decorated in the same manner as the daïs. The municipal band accompanied the Emperor to the Hôtel de Ville, playing national airs so far from melodious, that Napoleon quickly asked to be taken to his own room :

* See " Pièces Justificatives." Nos. 8, 9, and 10.

† It is worthy of remark that on the same day, and almost at the same hour, Louis XVIII. made his solemn entry into the capital.

but, on entering it, he found it so miserably furnished, that he immediately arranged with General Köller to have his sister Eliza's furniture sent from Lucca and Piombino. The General wrote to the authorities of the Grand-Duke of Tuscany, and they sent what was asked for, in a small vessel.

This fact gave rise to a false report which was circulated at the time, that Napoleon had seized upon a vessel belonging to his brother-in-law, and confiscated it, with its freight.

During the crossing, Captain Asher had been surprised to discover how much nautical knowledge Napoleon possessed. The Emperor greatly admired the severe discipline maintained on board the *Un-daunted*. "I did all that I could," said the Emperor, to Captain Asher, "to introduce a similar discipline into the French navy, but without success. The chiefs always would jest with their inferiors, and allow the sailors to play at cards and dominoes." Napoleon made himself very agreeable to the crew by his frank kindliness and by frequent tokens of his pecuniary generosity. On one occasion, while the sailors were dining, he approached them and tasted the dry peas which they were eating. Finding them detestable, he immediately gave one hundred francs to the canteen for wine for the men, and said, laughing, "If they cannot eat to my health, at least they shall drink to it."

Immediately after his arrival at the Island of Elba,

the Emperor visited the fortifications, and expressed his satisfaction that, by means of the improvements which he contemplated making, he should be able to defend himself against every kind of attempt on the part of the inhabitants of the continent.

General Köller remained ten days in the island, and completely gained the confidence of the Emperor, who consulted him in everything.

On several occasions, during their journey from France, he had said, "Your Majesty is wrong." Napoleon, who was little accustomed to such frankness, answered him sharply, "You are always telling me that I am wrong. Would you speak like that to your own Emperor?" The General assured him that his own Emperor would be very angry if he could suppose that he did not always speak his thoughts with candour. "In that case," replied Napoleon, "your master is much better served than I have ever been."

The Emperor occupied himself incessantly and most actively. Sometimes he would visit the little isles in the vicinity of the Island of Elba. Pianosa, the chief, and the most remarkable of these, boasts of extraordinarily rich vegetation, romantic sites, and troops of wild horses. At other times he would ride all over the island from end to end. With the plans which he had formed, if he had had time and strength to execute them, the prosperity of the island would have been doubled. In order to

gain the affection of the inhabitants, he had given
sixty thousand francs, shortly after his landing, for the
making of roads, which had been projected for a long
time, but never made for want of money.

Early in June, the Emperor had taken possession of
a house which was intended for the Commandant of
Engineers. This building was then composed of two
pavilions, united by a gallery, and is built upon a
rock overlooking the town of Porto-Ferrajo. Some
additions were made under his personal direction,
and the modest habitation became the residence of
him who had occupied by turns the palaces of all
the potentates of Europe, and who had left furniture
in his own palace to the value of over thirty to
forty millions. Madame Mère and Princess Pauline
soon arrived to inhabit a portion of the Emperor's
house. He gave up to them the rooms which he had
constructed between the two pavilions. Besides this
residence, Napoleon had a kind of villa at Rio. He
had also reserved for himself a mere lodging in the
Citadel of Porto-Longone, but he passed a part of each
day in a closed kiosk erected upon the top of a rock.
From thence he commanded the best perspective of
the seas, and in the hazy distance the coasts of Tuscany and the surrounding countries. Only Napoleon
ever entered this pavilion, to which the people gave
the name of *La Casa di Socrate.*

The four hundred men who had been allotted to
the Emperor for his guard, by the treaty of the 11th

of April, set out for Pithiviers, two days before his departure from Fontainebleau. They came through Lyons, where the officers were invited to a magnificent dinner by several young men of that city. The dinner took place at the famous restaurant of the Brotteaux.

They then crossed Mont Cenis, and, instead of going to Turin, repaired to Carmagnole and Savone. On their arrival at the latter port, General Cambronne sent an *aviso* to the Island of Elba, who arrived there in two days. The soldiery were embarked on four English vessels, and there were several days' delay before they sailed. Napoleon said that the interval which elapsed between the arrival of the *aviso* and that of the troopers was one of the most painful experiences of his life. The transports arrived on the 26th of May. The carriages and the draught and cavalry horses were all disembarked on the 27th without the slightest accident, by English sailors. Napoleon, who was on the spot, was greatly astonished at the way in which this was done. " Frenchmen," said he, " would have taken at least four days to do the same amount of work; all the vehicles would have been broken, and half the horses would have been lamed."

Some days after, Captain Asher left the Island of Elba. The Emperor, when he came to take leave, presented him with a gold snuff-box, in which his portrait, surrounded by twenty large diamonds, each of the value of 4500 francs, was set. I have been assured that Captain Asher refused 110,000 francs for this snuff-box.

The Emperor led a very active life at Elba. He always rose before daybreak, and devoted the early hours of the morning to work. Then came the review of his troops. This was not limited, as at the Carrousel, to a glance cast cursorily upon numerous corps. It was a minute inspection, and the military soul of Napoleon enjoyed it in all its details. Each grenadier was questioned as to his occupations, his habits, his health, and even his sentiments. The brave soldiers of the Isle of Elba sometimes had complaints to make. The Emperor gave them or promised them what they asked for, if the desired object was in his power; if not, he called them grumblers, pulled their moustachios, and walked away smiling.

In the evening, Napoleon went out riding, accompanied by his principal officers. Sometimes he received visits from foreigners of distinction, who came to the island in great numbers, merely to see him. Oftener still, he made fun with his staff of the abuse which was showered upon him by the French newspapers, which had flattered him before his fall, with the most shameless servility.

Thus were the days of the Emperor passed. Now at Porto-Ferrajo, now at Porto-Longone, or at Rio.

His Guard, after the fashion of the Roman warriors, helped in the greater part of the public works which he had set going in the island, and was daily

augmented by soldiers whose devotion to him led
them to join him. Napoleon could hardly maintain
this faithful battalion, nevertheless it grew and grew.
Some superior officers came to take service in it like
mere soldiers.

The abdication of Napoleon had been the result of
a treaty whose conditions were guaranteed by the
Allied Powers. Amongst other things, France was to
pay him an annual sum which had been defined. This
was never done. He learnt at the Island of Elba that
a project was being formed at Vienna to send him to
a distance from the coasts of France. It is said that
Talleyrand had represented his residence near the
coast as a source of constant disquietude, calculated to
inspire alarm, and embolden malcontents; and that he
ought to be placed at such a distance as to deprive
him of all hope of return. Add to his fear of this
being done, that he was without money—the little
that he had, proceeded from the sale of his mother's
diamonds,—and that, having claimed the execution of
the treaty, no answer was vouchsafed to him. Napoleon
made this breach of faith one of the pretexts for his
return. The true motive was necessity, and the
certainty of his being able to rally round him, by
showing himself, a considerable party belonging to
the military, to the purchasers of the national goods,
whose apprehensions concerning the security of their
acquisitions had already been most foolishly excited,
and all of those whose republican or revolutionary

principles rendered them inimical to the Bourbons.
He did not need either fighting troops or arms for
this enterprise. He needed only his person and his
fortune, which at first seemed to be about once more
to favour him.

Followed by eleven hundred men, whom he was
only enabled to pay by the aid of his mother, we all
know that he crossed France like a king re-entering
his States after an absence; that he had not to
burn a fuse; and that, up to the very moment of his
departure, not a soul but General Druot knew anything of his project. All the other persons learned it
at the moment of its execution. Napoleon himself
had not thought of it eight days previously; but the
private intimation which he received from Vienna,
that the question of transferring him to St. Helena
had been discussed at the Congress of Vienna, determined him to attempt this hazardous enterprise. I
have it from a man whose veracity cannot be doubted,
that, immediately after the departure of Napoleon
from the Island of Elba, some English travellers, who
happened to be there, visited the habitation which
had served him as a palace. They found his bedroom,
his cabinet, and his library in the same state in which
he had left them. The old woman, of Corsican origin,
who was the portress, was in the greatest anxiety,
not for herself, but for the safety and success of the
enterprise which her master had just undertaken.
The sincere attachment to him which she manifested,

all that she said, all that she related of the kindness
and gentleness which were habitual to him, afforded
the strongest refutation of the monstrous stories of
his private conduct, which were some time afterwards
given to the world. These travellers found a bath
still full of water, in the room next to Napoleon's bedroom, which proved that he had taken a bath as usual,
on the very morning of his departure, or at least the
night before. In his library, pieces of manuscript
paper, torn-up letters, and notes made in pencil, and
consequently not to be deciphered, were found lying
about in disorder. On the table was a map of France,
into which pins with large heads were stuck; and on
a small table, placed at the head of his bed, lay an
open volume of the History of Charles V., which he
had probably been reading on the eve of the day of
his embarkation.

CHAPTER XIX.

THE HUNDRED DAYS.

NAPOLEON'S RETURN TO FRANCE—HIS ARRIVAL AT PARIS—FOUCHÉ—THE CHAMP DE MAI—OPENING OF THE CAMPAIGN OF 1815—THE BATTLE OF LIGNY — WATERLOO — GENERAL ORNANO — NAPOLEON AT THE ELYSÉE—LUCIEN—THE CHAMBERS—THE SECOND ABDICATION OF THE EMPEROR—A PLOT—THE LAST SOJOURN AT MALMAISON NAPOLEON'S PROJECTS — HIS DEPARTURE FOR ROCHEFORT — HIS EXILE AT ST. HELENA—JOSEPH—PRINCESS PAULINE—QUEEN HORTENSE.

So little was Napoleon's return to France foreseen, that those who ought to have opposed it, taken unawares, had neither courage nor presence of mind. They abandoned the positions which had been entrusted to them, and left the field open to the Napoleonists and to the malcontents who swelled the escort with which the Emperor arrived at Paris. Seated for the second time, without any shock or commotion, upon a throne which he regarded as his own property, Napoleon committed the unpardonable fault of recalling the base flatterers whose vileness he ought then to have known well; or, rather, he had not the trouble of recalling them—they all came round him, and endeavoured by dint of fresh adulation to induce him to forgive their conduct at the time of his first abdication and his departure for the Island of Elba.

It was thought that Napoleon would make great concessions to those who were then called the "Independents," in order to conciliate them. They boasted of this, talked of the change of organization in the Chamber of Deputies, of the suspension of hereditary nobility, etc. Heads were turned by these ideas; liberty was talked of; and it was supposed that all these things were meant by the Champ de Mai. It took place. The Emperor's speech and the additional articles occasioned a general ferment. From that moment the sincere friends of Napoleon plainly foresaw that he was lost. Public opinion asserted itself. Notwithstanding the police, people talked, complained, and openly protested. Royalists and Independents joined together against him.

It is very likely that if Napoleon had known the state of things he would have made sacrifices to conciliate the public, but all those who surrounded him hid the truth from him, and paid spies of Fouché played a great part in this intrigue. It is a little-known fact that Savary, having learned a great deal that was very disquieting concerning Fouché, desired to impart it to Napoleon; but the latter made light of his revelations, which he attributed to Savary's jealousy at seeing Fouché in his place.

Savary was then in a kind of disgrace; the Emperor would not allow him to follow him at Waterloo, and showed him that he trusted him but little. The Duke had made the mistake of not going with his master to the Island of Elba, as he ought to have done; but he afterwards paid so dearly for his fault, that few persons will have the courage to reproach him with it.

Napoleon greatly desired peace, which he had so often refused, but he could not obtain it. All the Sovereigns feared him, and they united to re-establish Louis XVIII. The foreign armies received orders to march back towards the frontiers of France. Napoleon believed that his father-in-law would support him; he was ignorant of the intrigues by which Marie-Louise was surrounded, and hoped for her return. Persons who had come from Vienna did not dare to tell him the truth. M. de Menneval, who was so devoted and so faithful, was the only one who informed him that the Austrian Cabinet would oppose the return of the Empress, and even he did not dare to tell him to what she had pledged herself. The Empress, restrained by her plighted word, and deploring the weakness which had prevented her from following her husband to Elba, passed days and nights in grief. The Emperor, who had expected her, went on nevertheless with his war preparations; but he perceived, immediately on his arrival at Charleroi, that he no longer inspired his army or his generals with their former enthusiasm. The generals received him coldly, with discontent, and seemed to march with reluctance ; his Guard only, proved their devotion to him up to the last day. They sacrificed themselves for him, and enabled him to gain Paris, whither he went to place himself in the hands of his enemies.

Fortune having betrayed him in the field of Waterloo, Napoleon betrayed himself by abandoning his army. He might have rallied this army into a force all the more formidable that Marshal Gouchy's corps had not been touched. Nevertheless, the Parisians broke out into demonstrations of the greatest joy on the reception of the news that the French had gained a decisive battle at Ligny, under Fleurus, although no official details were received, and on the 19th of June a hundred and one guns were fired at the Invalides to announce this glorious intelligence. No bulletin arrived on that day, a circumstance which attracted no attention in the midst of the general joy; but when none appeared on the morrow, every one began to wonder and doubt, and there was visible disturbance in the places of public assembly. On the morning of the 21st, it was known that no news had arrived during the night, but at eleven o'clock a despatch from the Elysée-Bourbon gave rise to a rumour which converted the general alarm into joy. It was said that the Empress Marie-Louise had returned. One of my friends told me, on bringing me the news, that she had just made a visit to General Ornano, Napoleon's cousin, who was confined to bed by a wound which he

O

had received in a duel. She asked him if he knew the good news.

"Good news?" he replied.

"Yes, they say that the Empress has come back."

"The Empress!" he said, shaking his head, and showing her a little note he had just received; "you mean the Emperor? *for all is over.*"

An hour after my friend left the General, the news of the return of the Emperor was spread throughout the whole of the capital.*

Napoleon, on arriving at the capital, went at once to his brother Lucien, before entering the Palace of the Elysée. Lucien was for a moment overwhelmed by the narrative of the catastrophe, but, speedily regaining his presence of mind, he proposed to contend with events, disapproved his brother's having abandoned the army, advised him not to show himself in Paris, but to return in all haste and rally the remnant of his troops, and said to him with warmth, "You throw up the cards before the game is lost." In fact, it appeared to him to be still possible to unite the remains of the army of the North with that of the

---

* Authentic news of the fatal battle reached Paris about two hours before the return of Napoleon, and immediately on his arrival there was an assembly at M. de C——'s. The importance of forcing Napoleon to abdicate was being discussed, when, in the middle of the deliberations, a person entered the hall, and announced that the Emperor had returned. In a moment M. de C—— was left alone in his salon. The disputants were dispersed like bubbles on the surface of the water, or, rather, like frogs when a stone is thrown into the midst of them.—Communicated note.

Rhine, which was not yet engaged, and to oppose the imminent invasion with a new army, recruited by the Federates, and the National Guards of the various Departments of France.

But Napoleon already seemed incapable of taking any strong resolution, and a powerful party was about to prevail over that of his adherents on the spot. On entering the Elysée, Napoleon sent for the Minister of War, who found him in his bath and eating a plate of soup. Napoleon saluted him, and said : " I must have thirty thousand men and money." The Marshal's response not being satisfactory, the Emperor ordered the assembly of the Council. He had brought into Belgium twenty-six millions of francs, proceeding in part from his private purse, desiring to open the campaign magnificently, and to pay for everything that he required. Everything was seized by the Prussians, even to the Imperial carriages, the Coronation carriage included ; this had been brought up from Chambord, where it had been stored, I really don't know why.

Lucien still endeavoured to calm and reassure all in the Council of Ministers, which had been immediately convoked, and among the most prominent persons of the two Chambers. " This," said he, " is only the loss of a battle. Thirty thousand men *hors de combat* will not decide the destiny of France."

But fear had already taken possession of the hearts of the men of the 20th of March. Vainly did Lucien endeavour to revive their former courage. To some he pointed out the dangers of a cowardly desertion, to others he recalled what they had promised the Emperor eight days before he entered on the campaign. "Reverses," he added, "will not weaken our courage; they will but redouble our attachment to our Sovereign."

The question of dissolving the two Chambers was mooted in a private Council, but the firm and imposing attitude assumed by the Chamber of Deputies, secretly directed by Fouché, rendered all chance of success improbable. Recourse was then had to negotiations. The Ministers retained at the Palace of the Elysée, having received a second message which summoned them to repair to the Chamber, were authorized to do so by Napoleon. Lucien accompanied them in the character of Imperial Commissary, and required in his brother's name that the sitting should be formed into a private committee to receive important communications. The public immediately vacated the tribunes, and, the sitting having become private, Lucien read a message from his brother, containing a studied recital of the disaster which had just overwhelmed the army at Waterloo, without concealing its consequences. The Emperor recommended concert to the representatives, and announced the formation of a Commission composed of Carnot, Fouché, and Caulaincourt, to treat for peace with the Coalition.

The assembly kept a solemn silence for some minutes, but it was broken by the Deputy Henri Lacoste, who, measuring the depth of the ruin which Napoleon had brought upon France, said to the Assembly that only peace and energy could avail to save the country. Lucien, resuming his speech, endeavoured to justify his brother by trying to diminish the extent of the disaster, and represented that France was able to repair it. "The Emperor has several armies on foot," added he, "and all is not lost." A general murmur apprised him that the Assembly did not share his confidence. Then he employed all the resources of the art of oratory. He invoked the public generosity, and the respect due to men's oaths; he terminated his discourse by repeating the reproach of levity, so often addressed to the French nation. At these words, the indignation of the Assembly broke out. M. de la Fayette rushed into the tribune, and testified his astonishment that any one should dare thus to accuse the nation of levity. Addressing himself to Lucien as much by his gestures as by his words, he said, after a very animated speech: "Inform your brother that the nation will no longer have confidence in him; that we ourselves will undertake the salvation of the country, which he has delivered up to the wrath of Europe." Other orators indicated the same remedy. The Assembly having decided upon taking measures for the public safety on that night, Lucien and the

Ministers retired. In fact, notwithstanding the stead-
fastness of his friends, and even that of the patriots in
the two Chambers, Napoleon was none the less forced
to abdicate. That sacrifice was far from being voluntary on his part, as it has been said to be.

After the notification of his abdication to the
Chambers, on Friday, the 23rd of February, on which
day it was posted up in the capital, the emissaries of
the police discovered an organized plot to seize upon
the arsenals, arm the faubourgs, march to the Elysée
and re-establish the Imperial throne. The vigilance
of Fouché prevented the execution of this plan. All
the National Guard of Paris were under arms in the
evening, and so remained during the whole of the
night. No attempt at arrest was made, until a cannon,
fired close to the Barrière du Trône, had given the
signal of the conspiracy, and had revealed the chiefs
who advanced first to the place of rendezvous. They
were all taken, and nearly two hundred individuals
also arrested.

On the 24th of June, Napoleon retired to Malmaison, the cradle of his greatness. He had neglected
this dwelling, which recalled painful recollections to
him, especially since the death of Josephine. Its
melancholy salons received him again when he was
despoiled of his crown, but he came only to bid them
an eternal adieu.

The Emperor was not so much regretted by the
Government and the Chambers as might have been

supposed. Not only did they make no provision for him, but they even threatened Count Mollien, Minister of the Treasury, to have him brought to trial, for having disbursed certain sums for the private use of Napoleon. Since then, the Minister has declared that he did not give him a single franc, but he had already candidly acknowledged that he regretted to have been unable to succour the fallen Emperor in his great misfortune.

The first idea of Napoleon after his fall had been to retire to England, and this project may be regarded as a spontaneous homage rendered to the English nation, which he did not love, it is true, perhaps because he was forced to esteem it, but to which he believed he ought to do justice. He afterwards lent an ear to the proposition made to him that he should go to the United States of America. A number of American captains, who were then at Paris, offered him free ships; but Napoleon rejected everything which would have lent the appearance of flight to his departure. Being forced, however, to take a resolution, he decided in favour of the United States, and declared he was ready to leave France with his family for that destination. The Commission of the Provisional Government seemed to lend itself to the execution of this resolution. The Minister of Marine received orders to have two frigates ready to be placed at the disposal of Napoleon as he might require. Fouché knew that all this meant nothing. He was aware that a safe-conduct would have to be asked from Lord Wellington, and that it would not be granted. The Emperor was already the prisoner of England.

During this time the Austrians, the Russians, and the Prussians had, for the second time, arrived under the walls of Paris. The Emperor might be carried off from Malmaison. All was alarm around him. The few friends who remained to him intreated him to think of his safety. On the 29th of June the Commission of the Provisional Government, in its turn, hastened Napoleon's departure, and on the same day, at five o'clock in the evening, he left Malmaison. His suite was composed of Bertrand, Montholon, Gourgand, Savary, Lallemend, Las Cases, Planat, and Resigny. The Countess Bertrand accompanied her husband; M. Montholon also shared the hazardous destiny of hers.

The Emperor slept at Rochefort, where a courier was sent to him on the 30th, at daybreak. He opened the despatches which were handed to him, with emotion, and exclaimed after having read them, "It is all over; France is done for. Let us go." Napoleon paused no more until he reached Rochefort, where it was notified to him that he was to be exiled to the Rock of St. Helena. The rest is known.

Joseph, better advised, had profited by the offer of the American captains to take him to Boston. He arrived there without any difficulty.

On the 30th of June, Queen Hortense received an

order, rudely worded, and signed "Mouffling, Governor of Paris," to quit the capital within twenty-four hours and to leave the Kingdom of France with the utmost dispatch.

Lucien, who was convinced that Napoleon would not even escape from the Allies if he did not make up his mind to take refuge beyond the seas, had declared his own intention of retiring to the United States, whither all his family would have followed him. This resolution having been definitely arrived at between them, at the end of June, as I have said above, Lucien repaired to Neuilly to his sister Pauline's country house, and wrote a letter to apprise her of the new plans which had been formed between him and his brother.*

Each day the danger of the Imperial family became more imminent. Severe measures were taken by the Provisional Government against most of its members, and edicts of banishment, signed by M. de T——, had been notified to several former associates or colleagues of Napoleon. The moment had arrived when Lucien had to think of his safety. Under the name of Count de Chatillon, he took the road to Bordeaux, while the negotiations were going on with the Allied generals. He reached that post and hired a packet-boat, but, just as he was about to embark, he received intelligence of the fresh measures which had been taken against his brother, and of Napoleon's

---

* See "Pièces Justificatives," Nos. 11 and 12.

departure for Rochefort. This news made him suddenly change his resolution; for he was about to risk passing through England with the intention of obtaining the safe-conduct from the British Government which would be necessary to enable him to land in the United States. It will readily be supposed that he abandoned his intention.

CHAPTER XX.

SOME FEATURES OF NAPOLEON'S CHARACTER; VARIOUS ANECDOTES OF HIS LIFE, AND PARTICULARS RELATING TO THE PERSONS WHO FORMED THE IMPERIAL COURT.

THE GAME OF "BARS"—M. DE CAULAINCOURT—THE HOT PASTY—
M. DE MENNEVAL — THE ETIQUETTE OF THE COURT OF THE
TUILERIES — M. BARBIER — THE "MATERNAL SOCIETY" — M. TER-
NAUX — THE OLD AND THE NEW NOBILITY — THE DUKE OF PLA-
CENZA AND COUNT CHAPTAL — THE "GRAND SERVICE" AND THE
"PETIT SERVICE" — THE PASTIMES OF MARIE - LOUISE — THE
"PETITES ENTRÉES" — MESDAMES DE ROVIGO AND DE BOUILLÉ —
M. DE SAINT-AIGNAN—THE WHIP-STROKE AND THE SWORD-CUT—
THE BILLIARD-ROOM—THE EMPRESS'S ALBUM—COUNT DE LACÉPÈDE
—THE DUCHESS OF WEIMAR—MADAME BERTRAND.

I HAVE now only to add a few touches which will
serve to complete the portrait of Napoleon in his
private life. This was an aspect under which he was
little known, and has never been painted in true
colours. The same remark applies to the principal
personages of his family, and in general to all those
individuals who combined in lending that brilliancy
and splendour to the Imperial Court of which nothing
but the memory now remains.

While he was as yet only First Consul, Napoleon

frequently received writers, savants, and artists at his table. In the country he played at various games with them, especially at "Bars," a youthful pastime which he continued to enjoy, doubtless because it is an image of war. After he had been invested with the Imperial dignity, he considered that decorum forbade him to continue to act thus, and he limited himself to riding on horseback, which he liked very much, although he had several falls. One of these occurred one day at Trianon, when he was amusing himself by pursuing the Empress through the windings of a shrubbery. He jumped up at once, got into the saddle, laughing merrily, and rode off crying, "Casse-cou!"

I have seen him play at Bars after his marriage with Marie-Louise, and although he had already grown very stout, he still ran lightly. One day, when the Court was at Rambouillet, there was a great game of Bars, in which the Emperor fell twice, without hurting himself. He darted forward to seize his adversary, the Grand Marshal, who always slipped away from him, so that the Emperor was twice over sent rolling on the sand. He jumped up without a word, and went on with the game more gaily than before.

He liked luxury and magnificence on all public occasions; but he desired that strict economy should be maintained in his own house. Once, when on the way to Compiègne the horses were going more slowly than he liked, he let down the glass of the carriage, and called to the outrider in attendance, "Faster, faster!" M. de Caulaincourt, who, as Grand Equerry, preceded him in another carriage, heard this order, and, putting his head out of the window, shouted to the postillions, with an oath, that he would discharge them all if the pace was changed. The horses continued accordingly to go at a trot. On arriving at Compiègne, the Emperor complained of the slowness of the journey.

"Sire," answered M. de Caulaincourt, coolly, "give me more money for your stable expenses, and you may kill as many horses as you please."

Napoleon changed the conversation.

One day, when at breakfast with the Empress, he asked one of the first ladies who was in attendance what might be the cost of a hot pasty which was on the table.

"Twelve francs to your Majesty," she answered smiling, "and six francs to a bourgeois of Paris."

"That is to say that I am robbed!" exclaimed Napoleon.

"No, Sire; but it is the custom for a king to pay dearer than his subjects."

"That is just what I don't understand," said he, "and I mean to take order about it."

As a matter of fact, he entered into small details

of household economy which are often neglected by private individuals.

The same orderliness prevailed in the Empress's affairs. Each month the Countess de Luçay presented to her a statement of the expenditure of the preceding month; she signed it, and it was handed to M. de Ballouhai, Secretary of Expenses, whose duty it was to pay them. He had held the same office in the household of the Empress Josephine, and the Emperor, after his marriage with Marie-Louise, retained him in that capacity, as a reward for his perfect probity, his exactitude, and his attachment. M. de Ballouhai afterwards accompanied the Empress to Parma, where he received the most touching proofs of confidence and regard from her. The state of his health has since obliged him to return to Paris.

Napoleon's handwriting was always very bad, and latterly it was quite illegible. Only the secretaries who were accustomed to it could decipher it. In his signature it was impossible to distinguish anything beyond the three first letters, the rest was a random scrawl. Nothing could be more fatiguing than the post of First Secretary to Napoleon, which was filled by M. de Menneval for ten years. The Emperor then made him Secretary of Commands to Marie-Louise, and said to her, in presenting him, that M. de Menneval was the most estimable and the discreetest man he had ever known, but that he had worn him out with overwork. As a matter of fact, no night ever passed

without his sending for M. de Menneval to dictate
something to him, and he was frequently called several
times in the same night.

He subsequently proved that he deserved the high
esteem with which the Emperor honoured him. He
was placed in a difficult position at Blois and at
Orleans, for he was a witness of the intrigues with
which the Empress was surrounded, and he ventured,
without overstepping the bounds of respect, to lift up
the voice of truth. He never shrank from obeying
the suggestions of duty and affections. M. Fain,
who had been for a long time in the Emperor's service
as a secretary, took the place of M. de Menneval, and
displayed attachment and fidelity to the Emperor
which will do him immortal honour.

The physical organization of the Emperor was very
remarkable. He had the faculty of sleeping at will,
and this it was which enabled him to bear night-work
so easily. He generally went to bed at ten, rose
between one and two, worked until five or six, took
his bath, was dressed, received several persons, breakfasted at ten, then worked again until noon, when he
would come to his wife's apartment, or go out walking ;
but when business was urgent, he would stay at it
until evening. During the day he would come down to
see the Empress several times, and they would visit their
son together. If Napoleon had a little time to himself,
after he had kissed his wife and played with his child,
he would seat himself in an arm-chair, and, while still

talking, go fast asleep, waking only when he was told that some one or something was waiting for him.

He dined every day between seven and eight o'clock, alone with Marie-Louise. On Sundays there was a family dinner. Such was the etiquette of the Tuileries, from which there was no departure except in the case of Madame Lannes or Madame de Luçay, either of whom occasionally made a third at their Majesties' table.

On their short journeys, Napoleon every day invited three or four ladies, and as many men, but that honour was confined to certain persons.

When a petition was presented to him, he handed it to an aide-de-camp, or put it in his pocket. The latter meant that he would have it looked into. When he put the petition into his left pocket, which was called in the palace his " good " one, it was a sure sign that he was disposed to grant what was asked of him, even without the form of examination.

The Emperor had peculiar ideas and expressions of his own. One day, when he was talking with the Empress about some persons of whose conduct he did not approve, he said: " Chastity in a woman is what courage is in a man. I despise a coward and a woman without modesty ! "

Talking of Corvisart, the Emperor said he was an egoist ; that he had entrails but not " bowels."

The Empress protested against this, and said everybody was selfish, that she herself was selfish.

"Don't say, my Louise," said Napoleon gravely, " that you are selfish ; I know no more hideous vice."

Among the absurd stories circulated about the Emperor, those which imputed unbounded and revolting profligacy to him were most widely believed. I am about to cite two facts which will prove how much credit these inventions deserved.

The Emperor was very reserved with the ladies of the household, most of whom were of a staid age. Among the younger ladies, there was one who had some personal attractions, and whose head was filled with all the tales to which I have just alluded, so that her virtue was in a continual state of alarm. She meditated day and night upon her means of defence, prepared her speeches, and was resolutely determined to resist every kind of seduction, all sentiment, and even violence. With each day she expected the advent of the moment at which she would have to summon up all her resources ; she hardly dared to sleep ; at length she made up her mind to impart her fears to one of her companions. This lady, who understood the true state of affairs, begged her to calm herself, and to wait for the attack before troubling herself about the defence. As a matter of fact, the Emperor took no notice either of her or of the others, and she soon learned to laugh at her own terrors.

Napoleon was always angry when he saw novels being read. They were hidden when notice of his coming was given, but he frequently took the Empress's

P

readers by surprise. He had ordered his librarian, M. Barbier, to make a selection of books, and to send them to Marie-Louise. M. Barbier, who was rather a man of letters than a strict censor, included in his choice the Satires of Juvenal. The Emperor arrived just as we had received the books; he saw the Juvenal, and scolded vehemently about it, saying that young women had no business with such a book. He then informed us that, for the future, every book should pass through his cabinet; and, sending for his librarian, he lectured him severely.

I have been told by Madame Walewska, who honoured me with the title of her friend, and whom Napoleon always highly esteemed, that she breakfasted with him at Malmaison on the day before his departure for Rochefort, and that he was perfectly easy in his mind, even cheerful, and played for half an hour with her son, the little Alexander, with all his usual affection.

The Emperor was very fond of children. The pages looked upon him as a kind father, rather than an absolute master. He used the "tutoiement" towards them all, and called them by their Christian names. He had pet names for his particular favourites among them.

No one knew better than Napoleon what it was to be restricted in means. During the latter part of his sojourn at Elba, his Master of the Palace was obliged to cut down his table expenditure, by substituting the wine of the country for his Chambertin and his favourite Bordeaux. He consented willingly, and even laughingly, to this exercise of economy.

Officers of every nationality, who had served under him, came to his rocky realm, and were so earnestly desirous of being taken once more into his service, that, when he met them with the objection of the smallness of his means, some of them were content to receive from twenty to thirty-five sous a day, rather as a pledge of his esteem than as a recompense for their attachment. It is well known that, at St. Helena, he required to put in practice all the philosophy with which a man could be endowed by nature and experience; but even before his departure he had already regained entire tranquility at Malmaison, while his fate was still in uncertainty. At Elba, he invited Madame Bertrand's young family to dine with him almost every Sunday; and he seldom let her children leave him without making them some present, either of money or sweets, which he would put into his pockets for this express purpose. I do not think that such sentiments are incompatible with the outward appearance of indifference, and all the demonstrations of cold-heartedness, when the situation was such that it not only justified indifference, but even lent it an air of heroism.

Napoleon was deeply affected when he bade adieu to his mother and sister, on leaving the Island of Elba; so much so, that he said, "I must go now, or I shall never go."

In addition to what I have already said of Napoleon, I must relate a few anecdotes, and also give a denial to certain others which are entirely unfounded.

The following story gained extensive currency. It was said that the Emperor, in talking with Marie-Louise, complained of the Empress of Austria, and of the Archdukes, and that, after having expressed his displeasure with them, he added, "As for your father, I have nothing to say about him: he is a blockhead (*ganache*)." The Empress did not understand this word, and no sooner had Napoleon withdrawn than she asked the ladies who were with her what it meant. None of them ventured to tell her its true meaning, but one said that the word *ganache* signified a grave person, one of weight. The Empress forgot neither the expression nor the definition, and applied the word, some time afterwards, in a very amusing way, when she was acting as Regent of the French Empire. One day, while an important question was under discussion at the Council, she remarked that Cambacérès had not yet spoken. Turning towards him, she said—

"I should like to know your opinion on this subject, because I know that you are a *ganache*."

Cambacérès, on receiving this compliment, could only look at her with astonishment and confusion, repeating in an undertone the word "ganache!"

"Yes," said she, "a *ganache*, a cool-headed man, a man with sound sense. Is not that what it means?"

Nobody enlightened her, and the discussion was continued.

Of course it will be perceived at once that this anecdote is absolutely false. It is neither true nor likely. I have said elsewhere that Marie-Louise spoke and wrote French as well as the best-educated Parisian. I will add now, that I am quite sure Napoleon never used so slighting an expression in speaking of his father-in-law, with whom he had been very friendly for a long time. Besides, whenever he made any jests upon the house of Austria, Marie-Louise defended it with warmth. One day, for instance, when Napoleon was talking to his wife about the plans of the Emperor of Austria, for seizing upon certain towns which he wanted, he said:

"You see plainly that your father is a robber, and that he appropriates what does not belong to him."

"That is true," she replied: "but you steal kingdoms; my father takes only a few towns."

Napoleon laughed heartily at this answer, and asked the persons present whether a woman, who ought to respect her husband, had any right to call him a robber.

The Emperor, who was anxious to make Marie-Louise popular with the people, instituted the Société Maternelle, of which he made her president. Madame de Ségur was nominated vice-president; other ladies joined the Society. The object of the institution was to give aid to mothers of poor families having several children. They were attended in their confinements; provided with soup, wine, and clothes for their infants; and lastly, when they had several children, they were paid for nursing the latest born like ordinary nurses. Madame de Ségur filled her post in this institution with the kindness of heart, zeal, and intelligence which distinguished her, and she was the support and consolation of all the poor women who had recourse to her. Since the departure of Marie-Louise, this institution has been improved. The Duchess d'Angoulême, who was so charitable and munificent, became its president, and augmented its resources.

Napoleon wished his Court to be brilliant. A sure method of pleasing him was to have a well-regulated house, and elegant equipages, to give fêtes and receive on a large scale. He sometimes said, speaking of certain great personages, who were suspected of parsimony, "They are curmudgeons, who hoard up their money." He took great notice of the dress of the ladies. On coming into the salon he looked at each in succession, and his look was a regular inspection. He would go and say a gracious word to a lady whom he considered well-dressed, while one whose attire displeased him would be distinctly allowed to know it. He detested shawls, and no one could ever keep one on in his presence. The Cashmeres, which he put up with much against his will, and often talked about, displeased him still more. It was

in order to put them out of fashion that he ordered
some from M. Ternaux, designed by M. Isabey, which
were certainly prettier than the Indian ones. Nevertheless, the fashion still prevailed, and the latter
continued to enjoy the preference. Since then, they
have been perfectly imitated by M. Ternaux, and the
Emperor paid him a very high price for his first
attempts. He preferred diamonds for ornaments,
and nothing could surpass the brilliancy of the
spectacle at the Tuileries on a gala day. Even those
who were accused of avarice endeavoured to surpass
everybody else in diamonds. But "economizers"
were the constant objects of Napoleon's jests and
sarcasms. Sometimes they disregarded what he said,
but occasionally they got angry, and the only result
was to harden their resolution to save.

It was quite natural that there should be a great
disparity in a Court of such various material. The
old nobles, happy to find themselves once again at
their ease, freely enjoyed their fortune, sharing it
with all those who surrounded them, without for-
getting the poor. The newly enriched—princes, dukes,
counts, barons, etc.—emulated them in luxury, but
with less success. There were, however, some who
rose to the level of their rank, but the number was
small. Among the former were the Duke of Piacenza
and Count Chaptal. Many persons are unaware that
the former founded an establishment in the Department of Seine et Oise which gives employment to

more than three hundred families. It is a cotton-spinning factory, which he set up at Dourdan, in a very poor district, totally without resources. There now exists in that place a well-built village, called by its inhabitants Ville-Brun, from motives of gratitude to their benefactor. The Duke has, besides, established a primary school for children. Everybody knows what important services have been rendered to French industry by Count Chaptal, and the superb establishment which he has created at Chambord.

The Emperor knew every detail of what went on, and used to amuse himself by relating it all to the Empress. After his second marriage, he had a great desire to give his Court a better tone; above all, he was anxious to change its moral aspect, and to lend at least an appearance of propriety to everything Among the ladies who had been his favourites, only two preserved a place in his affections. One was Madame Walewska, who has always shown him a tender and faithful attachment; the other was a lady whose name I shall not disclose: up to the last moment the latter retained a certain influence over him.

The Princes and Princesses had ladies to accompany them. They formed their suite at the promenade, adorned the salon in the evening, and contributed by their conversation to the general amusement. In the case of the Queens these ladies were

called " dames du palais ;" in that of the Princesses,
" dames pour accompagner." These places were much
sought for, and almost all given by favour. Those
who obtained them were envied, because those who
desired them did not understand the disagreeables and
tribulations attached to them. Every three months
the list of " waits " was made out ; but it was a very
troublesome business to find the twelve ladies who
were required, some being ill, others absent, or in an
interesting situation. When, however, the list was
at length completed and the ladies nominated, they
arranged the order of waiting between themselves,
four to each month. Of these four, two only were on
duty every day ; the two others came in the evening,
and on Sunday. The two ladies whose waiting was
called the " grand service " appeared at eleven o'clock
in the morning, in the salon appropriated to them.
They were free either to occupy themselves, or to
do nothing, and remained there until one o'clock.
Then her Majesty went out, either in a carriage or
on foot. If on foot, they formed her suite. If it
happened (but this was very rare) that the Lady-in-
Waiting and the Lady of the Bedchamber were not
at the Palace, then the Empress took one of these
ladies in her carriage, generally the oldest or the most
important, and not the one whom she would have
preferred. But such fortune rarely befell them ; they
most usually followed in another carriage, with
the Gentleman-in-Waiting and a Chamberlain. The

Equerry and the Page on duty were always on horse-back, one on the right and the other on the left of her Majesty's carriage. The drive lasted one or two hours. On returning to the Palace the Empress bowed to these ladies, and went into her private apartments, followed by her Lady-in-Waiting and her Lady of the Bedchamber. The two ladies remained at the Palace until five o'clock. They then asked leave to retire, obtained it, and returned home, very tired, very much bored, very discontented, and very happy when nothing disagreeable had taken place. They had to come back at seven o'clock, and were not free until Marie-Louise retired to rest.

The evening was more agreeable than the day. The Emperor almost always asked for the suite; then the two ladies, the Chamberlain, the Equerry, and the Page came in. Nevertheless, I have seen a Duchess and a Countess who were on duty exposed to a very mortifying incident. All persons who had been pre-sented were admitted on the days of grand ceremonial, but a small number formed the private society of the Court. This was composed of the Ministers, the great dignitaries, and the favourites, both men and women. They had what is called the "petites entrées;" that is to say, the right of coming every day and at any hour. They all assembled in the same salon. When the Emperor had dined, he passed into his own salon, talked for a while alone with the Empress, all the doors standing open; afterwards he called for the

"entrées" and the suite. The Chamberlain repeated
the order, and each came in according to rank. If
he did not ask for the suite, then those who had not
the "petites entrées" remained in the first salon. These
"entrées" were given, and taken back, every three
months, so there should not be too many people at
once. One day that the Duchess of Rovigo and Madame
de Bouillé were "de grand service," the Emperor asked
only for the "entrées." The Chamberlain and the
Equerry only were there; they came in, and the two
ladies remained entirely alone. Madame de Bouillé
called for her carriage, and went away in a rage. The
Duchess, who was at least as much mortified, more
prudently remained; and this was well, for the Emperor,
being informed who were the ladies on duty that day,
hastened to say that they were to come in. The
Duchess only was to be found. She said that Madame
de Bouillé had been taken ill; but she was not believed,
and the Emperor loudly condemned the conduct of
the Countess. That evening he made himself very
agreeable to the Duchess of Rovigo.

In addition to the Ladies of the Palace, there were
several Chamberlains, some of whom were nominated by the Emperor to the service of the Empress.
The same was done with respect to the Equerries and
the Pages. There were four, and sometimes six, who
took their turn (I don't include among them Prince
Aldobrandini, her Majesty's First Equerry). Among
these Chamberlains and Equerries there was the same

mixture as elsewhere, and it would have been natural that the old nobility, thus socially united with the new, should give the tone and politeness of former times to the Imperial circle. This, however, was not the case ; and I must here remark, as several persons have done, that the old nobility affected the worst tone, and talked in the most indecent and unbecoming manner. These same individuals, on their return to the Faubourg St. Germains, would resume the habits and demeanour which they ought never to have laid aside. There were, however, some to whom this censure does not apply. In the service which he rendered to their Majesties, M. de Saint-Aignan united profound respect to all the graces of the mind, extensive information and fine manners. M. de M——— and M. d'E——— ought to have imitated him, but they did nothing of the kind. A disagreeable adventure occurred to the former. One day, when it was raining, he rode out of the Elysée Bourbon, by the side of the Empress's carriage, and, perceiving an individual who had kept his hat on his head, he struck the hat off with his whip, and flung it into the mud. The owner of the hat ascertained his name. A duel followed, and M. de M——— received a sword wound, which was fortunately not dangerous. He was blamed, and particularly by the Emperor, who expressed his displeasure at such conduct, adding, "It is very well done; he has only got what he deserved."

It will be surmised from what I have just

related, that the Ladies of the Palace, who were forced
by their service to pass five or six hours with these
gentlemen, did not find their society very pleasant,
and indeed they often complained of it. They were
obliged to listen to narratives of scandalous adventures, which made some of them blush, and embarrassed most of them ; they also had to endure very
unbecoming jesting upon their own affairs. The
Emperor was ignorant of all this. Before him everybody was respectful, polite, and reserved; but they
made up for that when his back was turned.

I must add, to finish what I have to say about
the salon, that a lady and two gentlemen played
cards with the Empress ; that other card-parties were
made up between the ladies, but in another room ;
and that the Emperor generally passed the evening in
talking with one or two of his Ministers, whom he
took into a little salon, where there was a billiard-
table for the Empress. Napoleon played billiards
very badly, without any attention, and ran about
the whole time: he chose that time to give vent
to his anger, or to scold, if he had anything to complain of. His voice only was heard, and he was
rarely answered. Indeed, except himself, nobody was
heard to speak in the salon ; although it was filled
with courtiers, it was impossible to distinguish any
voice. There was some talking, of course, but it was
carried on in very low tones, and according to the
usage of the old Court. The Emperor sometimes

played at whist, and he delighted in cheating, and laughed with all his heart when this was perceived, although nobody dared to make any observation to him on the subject.

Napoleon never relinquished friendships which he had formed in his youth. When he became First Consul, he continued to receive the friends of his humbler days at St. Cloud, with all his former familiarity. Of those who composed the Imperial Court, no one was more deserving of the esteem and friendship of honourable men than Count de Lacépède, the friend and worthy successor of the illustrious Bouffon, Grand Chancellor of the Legion of Honour from the foundation of that institution, and who lost his post on the arrival of Louis XVIII. at Paris. Count de Lacépède then retired to an estate which he possessed in the Department of Loire et Garonne.

When he was informed of the return of Napoleon, he did not hasten, like so many others, to grovel at the feet of his former master. He remained in his retreat, occupied by literary and scientific labours, until a courier came, bringing him the Emperor's order to resume his former functions, and also to preside over the Senate. Louis XVIII. had quitted France. The authority of Napoleon was recognized everywhere. It was his duty to render obedience to the summons. He therefore repaired to the post which was assigned to him. On the return of the King in the following year, he was a second time deprived of his functions.

and was, besides, struck off the list of senators. Nevertheless, no place was ever so well filled as that of Grand Chancellor of the Legion of Honour, while it was held by M. de Lacépède. He had the art of sending away even those whom he could not satisfy, well pleased. The Emperor had nominated him to the Seignory of Paris. This, with the Grand-Chancellorship, gave him a right to two separate salaries. For several years he refused to receive more than one, thus setting a good example of disinterestedness to the courtiers. What need had he of a great fortune? He had simple tastes, he lived without any display, and devoted every moment which he could spare from public affairs, to study. The venal men who surrounded Napoleon regarded his conduct with displeasure. They induced the Emperor to take a false view of it, and Count de Lacépède was ordered to receive his two salaries. He availed himself of this necessity to give freer course to his love of doing good. Among the numerous instances of those which I could relate, I shall limit myself to only one. A senior clerk, in the Bureau of the Legion of Honour, a highly respectable man with a family, had been ill for several months, and all the symptoms of his illness indicated that it was caused by mental anxiety. One of his intimate friends succeeded in discovering the secret, and learned that a debt of twenty thousand francs, contracted during the Revolution, for the subsistence of his family, still remained unpaid, and that

his creditor was threatening him every month with
a prosecution. This friend was acquainted with M.
de Lacépède, and, after having gravely reflected upon
the position of the sick man, he went to the Chancellor
and told him all, adding, that a person of his acquaintance, a man of merit and talent, would lend the
twenty thousand francs that were necessary, on the
sole condition that M. de Lacépède should give him
the place, if the senior clerk died before that sum of
money had been repaid. "That is impossible," replied
the Count, after a moment's thought. "I am very
sorry, but it would be unjust towards the under-clerk,
who has been doing his work since his illness, and
who deserves to have the place should so unfortunate
an event occur." The intercessor returned home ill
satisfied with the result of his attempt. Presently
a letter was brought to him from Count de Lacépède.
I give an exact copy of it.

"SIR,

"Have the goodness to hand to our friend
M. —— the accompanying trifle, and impress upon
him that he must not think of reimbursing me until
he has entirely recovered his health, and until he
possesses one hundred thousand livres a year.

"I am, etc.,

"B. G. E. L. V. S. COUNT DE LACÉPÈDE."

The "trifle" accompanying this letter was twenty
thousand francs in bank notes.

Everybody has heard how Napoleon, when a de-
spairing woman implored him to pardon her husband, burned in her presence a letter containing
the sole existing proof of his treason. The incident
is too well known to be related in detail. Another
of the same kind is less familiar. After the battle
of Jena, the French army commanded by Napoleon
was expected at Weimar. The most wealthy and
distinguished people of that city, especially the
ladies of the reigning family, fled to Brunswick,
because, as the Duke was serving in the Prussian
army with his troops, the vengeance of the conqueror
was to be dreaded. The Duchess alone resolved not
to abandon her capital. She retired into a wing of her
palace with her ladies, and caused apartments to be
prepared for the Emperor. On his arrival, the Duchess
left the little room which she had reserved for herself,
and took her place at the head of the grand staircase,
to receive him with all due ceremony.

"Who are you?" said Napoleon, on seeing her.

"I am the Duchess of Weimar."

"In that case I am sorry for you, as I shall crush
your husband."

He paid her no more attention, but retired into
the apartment prepared for him. The following
morning the Duchess learned that pillage had been
begun in the town. She sent one of her chamberlains
to the Emperor to inquire after his health, and
to ask for an audience. This proceeding pleased

Q

Napoleon, and he sent word to the Duchess that he should come and ask her to give him breakfast. Hardly had he arrived before he began, according to his custom, to question her.

"How could your husband, Madame," said he, "have been so foolish as to make war upon me?"

"Your Majesty would have despised him had he done otherwise."

"Why?"

"My husband has passed thirty years in the service of Prussia. It is not at the moment when the King had to contend against so powerful an enemy as your Majesty, that the Duke could forsake him with honour."

This answer, which was as adroit as it was just, seemed to soften the Emperor.

"But how came the Duke to attach himself to Prussia?"

"Your Majesty must be aware that the younger branches of the House of Saxony have always followed the example of the Elector. Now, the policy of the Prince having led him to ally himself with Prussia rather than with Austria, the Duke could not do otherwise than imitate the head of his house."

They continued to converse for some time upon the same subject, the Duchess still displaying equal intelligence and high spirit. At last Napoleon rose, exclaiming—

"Madame, you are the most estimable woman I

have ever known. You have saved your husband. I pardon him ; but it is to you alone that he owes it."

At the same time, he commanded the pillage in the town to be stopped, and order was restored there immediately. Some time afterwards he signed a treaty which secured the existence of the Duchy of Weimar, and he ordered the courier who was the bearer of it, to present it to the Duchess.

Since it has become the fashion to deny every kind of talent and every kind of merit to a man who has certainly conceived and executed extraordinary things, an effort has been made to deprive him of the glory of even his most brilliant actions. For instance, it has been said that the famous passage of the Bridge of Lodi was not an act of bravery, but a successful stratagem ; that the flag which he held in his hand when he flung himself upon the bridge was almost white, and that the enemy, taking it for a flag of truce, had suspended the fire during his passage. No more absurd fable could be imagined. To credit it we should have to suppose that the enemy were mad, or blind, if they could take for the bearer of a flag of truce an officer advancing towards them not alone, not even attended by a few men, but followed by a body of troops which occupied the whole breadth of the bridge, and came on at the charge. Among other things with which Napoleon has been reproached, is his answer to the Corps Législatif at the beginning of January, 1814. " In three months," he had said, "we shall have peace, the enemy shall be driven out, or I shall be dead." "Why did he not get himself killed?" asked certain persons. Perhaps he could not. All the officers who were with him in the neighbourhood of Troyes affirm that he exposed himself in such a way as to prove that he sought death.*

The following is a less known fact. In the various conflicts which took place around Brienne, the Emperor, aware of the resistance which he experienced, placed himself at the head of a squadron of Chasseurs, and joined the vanguard. There he led a succession of charges for two hours in the midst of a hail of balls. A young man whom I know has assured me that he and several others saw Napoleon fired at more than twenty times without being hit. His suite made incredible efforts to induce him to leave this dangerous post, but totally in vain; he seemed to be endeavouring to end his life. It would have been happy for him and for France if he had perished in the Plain of Champagne. We should not have seen the Hundred Days and the disasters which have followed them, nor he himself have endured captivity and humiliations to which death would have been far preferable.

My last words regarding Napoleon shall refer to his departure for St. Helena.

On his arrival at Rochfort, he still hoped that he

* "Perhaps he could not." Instead of these words, it would be more true to say that "death would have none of him." This is what he himself said at Fontainebleau.

could freely embark for America. He had been led to
believe this, but he found English vessels posted to
oppose his passage. There was in the port a Danish
barque, whose Captain had married a French woman;
and being touched by the Emperor's great misfortunes,
this man came to him and proposed to conduct him to
the United States if he would intrust himself to him.
He told him that there was a perfectly secure hiding-
place in his ship, but that it could only contain a
single man and some clothes, and he pledged his word
of honour that there Napoleon should be safe from
discovery. It is asserted that Napoleon was very
near accepting this offer, but the persons who accompanied him, fearing that it was only a snare,
did everything they could to prevent him. Napoleon
believed in the honour and generosity of the English
Government: the whole world knows how he was
treated.

The captivity of Napoleon at St. Helena; the
tortures of every kind which were inflicted upon him
by the Sovereigns, in revenge for his victories, and the
glory which he had had shed upon the French name;
the mean malice of the English Government,—all the
sufferings inflicted on this great man have obscured the
wrong done by his ambition. Every generous heart
was moved in his favour to compassion for the hero
struggling against a vile Governor, who was the im-
placable agent of the English Minister. Deep pity
was felt for the husband, the father, separated not

only from his wife and from his son, but also from his mother and his sisters, by whom he was so dearly loved, and who were refused permission to join him. Had anything more been needed to revive the love of Napoleon and hatred of his oppressors in the hearts of the French, his death has augmented these two sentiments. No fact exists in history comparable to the emotion with which his ashes were received. All France crowded the route over which the coffin passed, following it with enthusiasm, saluting it with shouts until the moment of its arrival at the Invalides. Thenceforth, for years, there was an incessant crowd eager to look upon his tomb. Napoleon alone has had such a triumph after his death. All honour be to him who claimed those ashes, and likewise to him who brought them back to France!

APPENDIX.

No. 1.

A Report made to the Corps Législatif, by the Extraordinary Commission appointed by that Body, on the 28th of December, 1813 :—

GENTLEMEN,

The Extraordinary Commission which you have appointed, in virtue of the Emperor's decree of the 20th of December, 1813, presents the Report which you are expecting under these grave circumstances.

It is not for the Commission only, it is for the Corps Législatif as a whole, to express the sentiments which are inspired by the communication of the original documents in the custody of the Ministry of Foreign Affairs, by command of his Majesty. That communication has taken place under the presidency of his Serene Highness the Arch-Chancellor of the Empire. The documents which have been placed before us are nine in number.

Among these documents are notes, by the French Minister and the Austrian Minister, which date back to the 18th and 21st of August.

They also include the speech delivered by the Regent to the English Parliament, on the 5th of September. The Regent said—

" It is not within the intentions of his Majesty, or within those of the Allied Powers, to demand from France any sacrifice which may be incompatible with her honour and her just rights."

The present negotiation for peace begins with the 10th of last November. It was arranged by the agency of the French Minister in Germany. Having been present at an interview between the Ministers of Austria and England, he was commissioned to carry back the words of peace to France, and to make known the general and compendious bases upon which peace might be negotiated.

The Minister of Exterior Relations, M. le Duc de Bassano, replied, on the 16th, to this communication from the Austrian Minister. He stated that a peace founded on the basis of the general independence of nations upon both land and sea was the object of the desires and the policy of the Emperor; in consequence, he proposed that a Congress should be assembled at Manheim.

The Austrian Minister replied, on the 23rd of November, that their Imperial Majesties and the King of Prussia were ready to negotiate, as soon as they should have received an assurance that the Emperor of the French admitted the general and compendious bases previously communicated.

The Powers hold that the principles contained in the letter of the 16th, although generally shared by all the Governments of Europe, could not take the place of bases.

On the 2nd of December, the Minister of Exterior Relations, M. le Duc de Bassano, gave the desired assurance.

Recapitulating the general principles of the letter of the 16th, he announces, with lively satisfaction, that his Majesty the Emperor gave his adherence to the proposed bases, that these would involve great sacrifices on the part of France, but that she would make those sacrifices without reluctance, in order to give peace to Europe.

To this letter the Austrian Minister replied, on the 10th of December, that their Majesties had learned, with satisfaction, that the Emperor had adopted the essential bases of the balance of power and the tranquility of Europe, that they had given orders for the communication of the document to their Allies, and did not doubt that negotiations might be opened immediately after their answers.

According to the communications which have been made to us, the negotiation stops with this latter document.

With that document it is permissible to hope it

will resume its natural course, when the delay, rendered necessary by a more distant communication, shall be over. It is, then, upon these two documents that our hopes may rest.

While this correspondence was taking place between the respective Ministers, there was printed, in the *Frankfort Gazette*, and placed before your Commission, in virtue of the close letter of his Majesty, a declaration of the Allied Powers, under date of the 1st of December, in which, among other things, the following passage is to be remarked :—

" The Allied Sovereigns desire that France may be great, strong, and fortunate, because the greatness of the French power is one of the fundamental bases of the social edifice. They desire that France may be fortunate, that French commerce may revive, that the Arts —a gift of peace—may flourish afresh, because a great people can only remain quiet in proportion to its prosperity. The Powers confirm to France an extent of territory which she never knew under her kings, because a brave nation is not a fallen one for having, in its turn, sustained reverses in a stubborn and sanguinary conflict, in which it has fought with its accustomed intrepidity."

It results from these documents that all the belligerent Powers have plainly expressed a desire for peace.

You have especially observed therein that the Emperor has manifested a resolution to make great

sacrifices, that he has acceded to the general and compendious bases proposed by the Allied Powers them
selves.

The most patriotic anxiety does not require that
those general and compendious bases should as yet
be made known.

Without seeking to penetrate into Cabinet secrets,
when the knowledge of them is not necessary for the
object to be attained, is it not sufficient to know that
those bases are only the conditions desired for the
opening of a Congress ? Does it not suffice to remark
that those conditions have been proposed by the Allied
Powers themselves, and to be convinced that his
Majesty has given his full adherence to the bases
necessary to the opening of a Congress in which all
rights and all interests are to be discussed ? The
Austrian Minister has, besides, acknowledged that the
Emperor had adopted bases essential to the restoration of the balance of power in Europe, and consequently the adherence given by his Majesty to those
bases has been a great step towards the pacification
of the world.

According to the Constitutional regulations, it is
the province of the Corps Législatif to express the
sentiments to which these communications give rise ;
for it is enacted by clause 30, of the Senatus-con-
sultum of the 18th Frimaire, Year XII., that—

"The Corps Législatif, on every occasion when the
Government shall make a communication to it, on any

other subject than the voting of a law, shall form itself into a general committee to deliberate upon its answer."

As the Corps Législatif expects its Commission to offer reflections appropriate to the preparation of a response worthy of the French nation and of the Emperor, we take leave to express some of our sentiments to you.

The first is that of gratitude for a communication, which at this moment summons the Corps Législatif to take cognizance of the political interests of the State.

We experience a feeling of hope, in the midst of the disasters of war, on seeing kings and nations emulating each other in pronouncing the name of peace.

In fact, gentlemen, the solemn and reiterated assurances of the belligerent Powers agree with the universal desire of France for peace, with that desire which is generally expressed around each one of us in our respective departments, and which finds its natural organ of expression in the Corps Législatif.

According to the general bases contained in the declarations, the desire of all humanity for a firm and honourable peace would seem to be about to be realized speedily. It will be honourable, because, for nations as for individuals, honour consists in the maintaining their own rights and respecting the rights of others. That peace will also be firm, because the true guarantee of peace is the interest which each of the contracting parties has in remaining faithful to it.

What, then, can hinder and retard its blessings? The Allied Powers bear the striking testimony to the Emperor that he has adopted the bases essential to the restoration of the balance of power and the tranquility of Europe.

We have, as the first pledge of his pacific intentions, Adversity, that true counsellor of kings, the plainly expressed need of the people, and even the interest of the Crown.

To these pledges you will, perhaps, think it useful to entreat his Majesty to add one still more solemn.

If the declarations of the foreign Powers were fallacious, if they desired to enslave us, if they meditated the rending asunder of the sacred soil of France, it would be necessary, to prevent our country from becoming the prey of the foreigner, to render the war national; but, in order the more securely to effect that righteous operation which saves empires, is it not necessary to unite the nation and its monarch in closer bonds?

It is a necessity to impose silence upon our enemies respecting their accusations of aggrandizement, of conquests, of alarming preponderance. Since the Allied Powers have thought it their duty to reassure the nations by publicly proclaimed protestations, is it not worthy of his Majesty to enlighten them by solemn declarations, upon the designs of France and the Emperor?

When that Prince to whom history has preserved the name of "Great" wanted to rekindle the spirit of his people, he revealed to them all that he had done for peace, and his high confidences were not without effect.

Would there not be real greatness in disabusing the Allied Powers, in order to prevent them from accusing France and the Emperor of desiring to hold too extensive a territory, whose preponderance they seem to dread?

It is not, indeed, for us to inspire words which would resound throughout the universe; but in order that the declaration might have a useful influence upon the foreign Powers, and produce the hoped-for influence in France, would it not be desirable that it should proclaim to Europe and to France a promise not to continue war except for the independence of the French people and the integrity of their territory?

Would not this declaration have an indisputable authority in all Europe?

When his Majesty should thus have replied, in his own name and in that of France, to the declaration of the Allies, there would be seen, on the one side, the Powers who protest that they do not want to appropriate to themselves a territory recognized by him as being necessary to the balance of power in Europe, and, on the other, a monarch which would declare himself to be animated solely by the resolution to defend that territory.

That, if the French Empire only remained faithful to those liberal principles, which, however, the chiefs of the nations of Europe have all proclaimed, France would then, being forced by the obstinacy of the enemy to a war of the nation and of independence, to a war of acknowledged justice and necessity, be capable of displaying energy, unity, and perseverance in support of her rights, she has already given sufficiently striking proofs. Unanimous in her desire to obtain peace, she will be equally unanimous in her efforts to conquer it; and she will again show the world that a great nation can do all it wills, when it wills nothing except that which its honour and its just rights demand.

The declaration, for which we venture to hope, would meet the views of the Powers who do homage to French valour; but this is not enough to rally the nation itself and to put it into a state of defence.

It is, according to the laws, for the Government to propose such means as it believes to be surest and speediest for repulsing the enemy and securing a firm and lasting peace.

Those means will be effectual, if the French are convinced that the Government aspires to the glory of Peace only; they will be effectual, if the French are convinced that their blood will be shed solely in defence of their country and of protecting laws; but those consoling words "country" and "peace" would resound in vain if the institutions which promise the benefits of both one and the other be not guaranteed.

It appears, therefore, indispensable to your Commission that, when the Government shall propose the promptest measures for the safety of the State, his Majesty shall be, at the same time, entreated to maintain the entire and constant execution of the laws which guarantee to Frenchmen the rights of liberty, security, and property, and to the nation the free exercise of its political rights. This pledge appears to your Commission the most effectual means of restoring to the French people the energy which is needed for their own defence.

These ideas have been suggested to your Commission by the desire and the necessity for binding the throne closely to the nation, in order to make combined efforts against arbitrary anarchy and the enemies of our country.

Your Commission has limited itself, according to its functions, to laying before you reflections which have appeared to it appropriate to the preparation of the answer which you are called upon to make by the Constitution.

How will you convey it? The Constitutional regulation determines the method: it is by discussing your answer in general committee; and as the Corps Législatif is called upon to present an address each year to the Emperor, you will probably think fit to adopt that mode of conveying the answer to the communication which has been made to you. If his Majesty's first thought, in important circumstances, has been to collect the deputies of the nation around the throne, is it not their first duty to make a fitting response to that convocation by letting the truth, and the people's desire for peace, be known to the monarch ? *

No. 2.

Napoleon's Speech to the Deputation from the Corps Législatif, January 1, 1814.

GENTLEMEN,

I called you together that you might assist me to do good; you have disappointed my expectation. You have allowed yourselves to be led by five factious persons.

M. Lainé is a mischievous man. I know that he maintains relations with the Regent of England, through the medium of De Séze, the lawyer. M. Raynouard has said that General Masséna committed vile and base acts in a certain château: he has lied. The imputation cast on the General is a calumny. How comes it that a Marshal of the Empire is treated in such a fashion? I know how all numerous assemblies are led: one gets into this corner, another into

---

* At St. Helena the Emperor declared this document to be incorrect, and that, as it was reported, it was not reasonable. As Napoleon did not indicate the passages which were not correct, I give the report, with his observation.

R

that, and presently the whole mass follows the impulse that it has been given.

Among you, eleven-twelfths are honest people, but there are also schemers and agitators; I know them. In the Corps Législatif there are worshipful magistrates, procurators-general, judges, notaries, an Envoy Extraordinary to the United States; but intrigue has dictated your choice. The same men appear on the Diplomatic Commission, on the Finance Commission, and on the Commission for drawing up the Address.

The Report of your Commissions has given me great pain; I would rather have lost two battles. To what did it tend? To augment the claims of the enemy! It proposed that I should yield more than the enemy exacts. If they were to demand Champagne Brie, I should then have to give up also? Yes, a frank declaration of my sentiments was desired; I have made it: we will no longer fight to make or to keep conquests, but only to deliver France.

If abuses have been committed, I ought to have been told of them, division by division. I should have put my Commissaries in communication with my Ministers; they would have verified those abuses. We should have washed our dirty linen at home. But is it in presence of the enemy that these remonstrances ought to have been made? The object of them was to humiliate me. It was designed to throw dirt in my face. I may be killed, but none shall dishonour me.

I was not born among the kings, and I care not for the throne. What is a throne? Four bits of gilded wood, covered with a length of velvet. A thousand woes surround thrones; but while I sit on one, I will defend its rights. The nation has more need of me than I of it.

Your Commission has humiliated me more than the enemy did; it has said that Adversity is the truth-telling counsellor of kings; and that thought is a true one, but the application that is made of it is cowardly. My enemies have never reproached me with not being above adversity; to do so is to add irony to insult.

In four months, I shall publish the odious Report of your Commission. If any one thinks proper to circulate it, I shall have it printed in the *Moniteur*, with notes from my own hand.

What did you want to do? To carry us back to the Constitution of 1791? I will not have a constitution about which I understand nothing. If Louis XVI. had not accepted it he would be reigning still.

Did you reckon the faubourgs Saint-Antoine and Saint-Marceau? Did you want to imitate the Legislative Assembly? It allowed itself to be governed by the Girondists, by Verguiaux, Guadet, and the rest. What has become of them? They are in the grave.

Who are you, to reform the State? You think you are the representatives of the nation. In England the Commons are representatives, because they are nominated by the people: our Constitution is not the same; that is not my fault. You are only deputies to the Corps Législatif. The real representative of the nation is I, who have been three times proclaimed their Sovereign by four millions of citizens. The Senate and the Council of State share the legislative power with me, and before you; every authority is attached to the throne, all is in the throne.

I repeat, that more than eleven-twelfths of you are good; but you have let yourselves be led by factious men. M. Lainé is a traitor; I shall keep an eye upon him and the evildoers, and I will repress them.

Return to your Departments. I count upon the good spirit which you will take back thither. Tell your fellow-citizens that the resources of France are not so much exhausted as it is supposed. If I again meet with reverses, I will await my adversaries in the plains of Champagne. In three months we shall have peace; the enemy will be driven out, or I shall be dead.

No. 3.

The Emperor Napoleon's Act of Abdication.

THE Allied Powers having proclaimed that the Emperor Napoleon was the sole obstacle to the restoration of peace in Europe, the Emperor Napoleon, faithful to his oath, declares that he renounces, for himself and his heirs, the throne of France and of Italy, and that there is no personal sacrifice, even that of life, which he is not ready to make to the interest of France.

(Done at the Palace of Fontainebleau, on the 11th of April, 1814.)

(Signed) NAPOLEON.

(Countersigned) DUPONT (of Nemours),

Secretary-General of the Provisional Government.*

No. 4.

The Speech addressed by Napoleon at the Moment of his Departure, to the Troops of the Old Guard who had remained with him.

OFFICERS, subalterns, and soldiers of my Old Guard, I bid you farewell.

For the twenty years that I have commanded you, I have been well pleased with you; I have always found you on the path of glory.

The Allied Powers have armed the whole of Europe against me; one portion of the army has forsaken its duty, and France has yielded to private interests.

With you and the brave men who have remained

* I have been told that after Napoleon had executed this deed, he displayed the utmost calmness, the noblest resignation, and that he seemed like one relieved of a heavy load. He talked, a few minutes afterwards, familiarly and like any ordinary citizen, with the general officers of his Court, about the results of the Revolution, as though it had nothing to do with him, and made a long allocution to them full of generous sentiments.

faithful to me, I could have carried on civil war for three years; but France would have been unhappy, and that would have been contrary to the aim which I have incessantly kept before me. It was, then, my duty to sacrifice my personal interests to her happiness : I have done so.

My friends, be always faithful to the new Sovereign whom France has just chosen for herself; do not forsake that dear country, too long unhappy. Do not lament my fate ; I shall always be happy in knowing that you are so. I might have died, nothing could have been easier to me; but no ! I shall always follow the path of honour. I will write what we have done !

I cannot embrace you all, but I am about to embrace your chief. Come, General ! [He embraced General Petit.] Bring me the eagle. [While embracing it, he said] Dear eagle, may these kisses resound in the hearts of all my brave men.

Farewell, my children ! Adieu, my friends ! Come round me once more !

No. 5.

It was only for the purpose of counteracting the effect of the "Address of the Provisional Government to the Army," upon the mind of his troops, that Napoleon put forward the following "Order of the Day," which was dated the 4th of April, 1814 :—

THE Emperor thanks the army for the attachment
which it manifests to him, and principally because it
recognizes that France is in him, and not in the people
of the capital. The soldier follows the fortune and
the misfortune of his general, his honour and his
religion. The Duc de Ragusa did not inspire his
companions in arms with those sentiments. He has
gone over to the Allies. The Emperor cannot approve
the condition under which he has taken this step; he
cannot accept either life or liberty from the mercy of
a subject. The Senate has permitted itself to dispose
of the French Government: it has forgotten that it
owes the power which it now abuses to the Emperor;
that it is he who saved one part of its members from
the storm of the Revolution, and who took the other
part out of obscurity, and protected it from the enmity
of the nation. The Senate avails itself of the Articles
of the Constitution to overturn it; it unblushingly
reproaches the Emperor, regardless of the fact that, as
the first Body of the State, it has taken part in all the
events that have occurred. It has gone so far as to
dare to accuse the Emperor of having changed certain
Acts in publication: the whole world knows that he
had no need of such artifices; a sign was an order for
the Senate, which always did more than was desired
of it. The Emperor has always been accessible to the
wise remonstrances of his Ministers, and he expected
from them, in that circumstance, a most definite jus-
tification of the measures which he had taken. If

enthusiasm was admitted into the public speeches and addresses, then the Emperor has been deceived; but those who spoke in such a fashion ought to attribute the fatal result of their flattery to themselves. The Senate does not hesitate to speak of libels published against foreign Governments; it forgets that they were concocted within itself. If these men remained faithful so long as fortune was constant to their Sovereign, and no complaint of the abuse of power was ever heard; if the Emperor did despise men, as he is reproached with despising them, the world will acknowledge now that he had reasons which justified his contempt. He held his dignity from God and from the nation; they alone could deprive him of it. He has always regarded it as a burden, and when he accepted it, he did so with the conviction that only he could carry it worthily. Good fortune seemed to be his destiny; now that fate has decided against him, the will of the nation alone could persuade him to remain longer upon the throne. If he must regard himself as the only obstacle to peace, he readily makes the last sacrifice to France. He has therefore sent the Duc de Moskowa to Paris to open negotiations. The Army may be certain that its honour will never be in opposition to the welfare of France.

No. 6.

Treaty between the Allied Powers and his Majesty the Emperor Napoleon.

ARTICLE I.—His Majesty the Emperor Napoleon renounces, on behalf of himself, his successors and descendants, as well as on behalf of all the members of his family, all rights of sovereignty and dominion over the French Empire, the Kingdom of Italy, and every other country.

Article II.—Their Majesties the Emperor Napoleon and Marie-Louise shall retain their titles and rank, and enjoy them during their lifetime. The mother, brothers, sisters, nephews, and nieces of the Emperor shall also retain, in whatsoever place they reside, the titles of Princes of his family.

Article III.—The Island of Elba, which the Emperor Napoleon has chosen as his place of residence, shall form, during a life, a separate principality, which he shall hold wholly as his property and his sovereignty. There shall also be granted to the Emperor Napoleon an annual revenue of two millions of francs, as his absolute property, which shall be charged as an annuity upon the Great Book of the Public Debt. Of this sum one million of francs shall be reversionary to the Empress.

Article IV.—The Duchies of Parma, Piacenza, and Guastalla shall be given wholly as property and sovereignty to her Majesty the Empress Marie-Louise; they shall pass to her son and to his descendants in the direct line. The Prince, her son, shall take in future the title of Prince of Parma, Piacenza, and Guastalla.

Article V.—All the Powers undertake to use their good offices with the States of Barbary to secure respect for the flag of Elba, and with that purpose their relations with those States shall be assimilated to those of France.

Article VI.—There shall be reserved, in the territories which by these presents he has renounced, to his Majesty the Emperor Napoleon, for himself and his family, domains or annuities upon the Great Book of the Public Debt, producing a revenue of two millions five hundred thousand francs, free of all charges and deductions. These domains or annuities shall belong entirely to the Princes or Princesses of his family, who may dispose of them as they shall think proper. They shall be so shared among them that each shall have following revenues :—

Madame Mère, 300,000 francs; King Joseph and his wife, 500,000 francs; King Louis, 200,000 francs; Queen Hortense and her children, 400,000 francs; King Jérôme and his wife, 500,000 francs; the Princess Elisa (Bacciochi), 300,000 francs; the Princess Pauline (Borghese), 300,000 francs.

The Princes and Princesses of the house of the Emperor Napoleon shall retain, as well, the real and personal property of every kind whatsoever, which they shall possess by public and individual right, and the annuities which they shall also enjoy (as individuals).

Article VII.—The pension of the Empress Josephine shall be reduced to a million in domains, or in inscription upon the Great Book; she shall continue in the sole possession of her property, both real and personal, with power to dispose of it in accordance with the laws of France.

Article VIII.—A suitable establishment shall be formed out of France for Prince Eugene, Viceroy of Italy.

Article IX.—The property which the Emperor Napoleon possesses in France, whether in extraordinary domains, or in special domains attached to the Crown of France; in funds placed by the Emperor, either on the Great Book of the Public Debt, or in the Bank of France, in Forest share, or in any manner whatsoever, and which his Majesty resigns to the Crown, shall be reserved as capital, which shall not exceed two millions, to be employed in donations to persons whose names shall be inscribed upon a list signed by the Emperor Napoleon, and which shall be transmitted to the Government.

Article X.—All the Crown Jewels shall remain in France.

Article XI.—His Majesty the Emperor Napoleon shall replace in the Public Treasury, and the other depositaries, all the sums which shall have been taken from them by his command, with the exception of that which has been appropriated to the Civil List.

Article XII.—The debts of the household of his Majesty the Emperor Napoleon, such as they existed on the day of the signature of the present treaty, shall be paid out of the arrears due by the Public Treasury to the Civil List, according to the estimate which shall be signed by a commission nominated for the purpose.

Article XIII.—The obligation of the Mont-Napoléon of Milan (Mont-de-Piété) towards creditors, French or foreign, shall be discharged, unless it should be otherwise ordained hereafter.

Article XIV.—All the necessary passports shall be delivered to allow free passage to his Majesty the Emperor Napoleon, the Empress, the Princes, the Princesses, and all the persons of their suite who shall desire to accompany them, or to establish themselves out of France, as well as for their equipages, horses, and effects. Consequently, the Allied Powers shall furnish officers and troops to escort them.

Article XV.—The Imperial French Guard shall furnish a detachment of from twelve to fifteen hundred men of all arms, to serve as an escort to his Majesty the Emperor Napoleon, so far as Saint-Tropez, the place of his embarkation.

Article XVI.—A corvette and the necessary vessels shall be furnished for the transport of his Majesty the Emperor Napoleon and his household; and the corvette shall belong wholly to his Majesty the Emperor.

Article XVII.—The Emperor Napoleon shall take with him, and retain as his Guard, four hundred men —officers, subalterns, and volunteer soldiers.

Article XVIII.—No Frenchman who shall have accompanied the Emperor Napoleon, or his family, shall be held to have lost his rights as a Frenchman by not returning in the course of three years; at least he will not be comprised in the exceptions the making of which the French Government reserves to itself after that term.

Article XIX.—The Polish troops of all arms shall be at liberty to return to Poland, and shall keep their arms and baggage as a testimony to their honourable services. The officers and soldiers shall retain the decorations which they have obtained, and the pensions that are attached to them.

Article XX.—The High Allied Powers guarantee the existence of the present treaty, and pledge themselves to obtain that it be accepted and guaranteed by France.

Article XXI.—The present Act shall be ratified, and the ratifications exchanged at Paris in two days.

Done at Paris, the 12th of April, 1814.

(Signed) METTERNICH, STADION, RASOU-MONSKY, NESSELRODE, CASTLE-REAGH AND HARDENBERG, NEY AND CAULAINCOURT.

No. 7.

The Proclamation of Marshal Augereau to his Troops.

SOLDIERS,

The Senate, the interpreter of the National will, *weary of the tyrannical yoke of Napoleon Buonaparte,* pronounced his fall (*déchéance*), and that of his family, on the 2nd of April.

A new monarchical constitution, strong and liberal, and a descendant of our former kings, replace *Buonaparte* and *his despotism.*

Your grades, your honours, and your distinctions, are secured to you.

The Corps Législatif, the great dignitaries, the Marshals, the Generals, and all the Corps of the Great Army have given their adherence to the decrees of the Senate, and *Buonaparte* has abdicated the thrones of France and Italy, on behalf of himself and his heirs, by an Act, dated the 11th of April, at Fontainebleau.

Soldiers, you are released from your oaths; you are released by the nation in which sovereignty resides; *you are again released, were it necessary, by the abdication of a man who, after having immolated millions of victims to his cruel ambition, has not been capable of dying like a soldier!*

The nation calls Louis XVIII. to the throne. He is a Frenchman born; he will be proud of your glory and

will surround himself with your chiefs: a descendant
of Henry the Fourth, he will have the heart of his
ancestor, he will love the soldier and the people.

Let us, then, swear fidelity to Louis XVIII. and to
the Constitution which presents him to us; let us
hoist the true colour of France, before which every
emblem of a revolution which is ended disappears;
and you will soon find a just recompense for your
noble deeds, in the gratitude and the admiration of
your King and country.

MARSHAL AUGEREAU.

Head-quarters, Valence, 16 April, 1814.

No. 8.

The following proclamation was issued, as I have
said, by order of General Dalesme; I have been assured
that it was chiefly drawn up by himself:—

INHABITANTS OF THE ISLAND OF ELBA,

Human vicissitudes have brought the Emperor Napoleon into your midst; and his own choice
gives him to you as your sovereign. Before entering
within your walls, your august and new monarch has
addressed the following words to me, and I hasten to
impart them to you, because they are the pledge of
your future welfare :—

"General! I have sacrificed my rights to the interests of the country, and I have reserved to myself

the sovereignty of the Island of Elba, which has been consented to by all the Powers. Be so good as to make this new state of things known to the inhabitants, and the choice which I have made of their island for my abode, in consideration of the mildness of their manners and their climate. Tell them that they shall be the constant objects of my warmest interest."

Elbese! these words need no comment; they fix your destiny. The Emperor has judged you rightly. I owe you this justice, and I render it to you.

Inhabitants of the Island of Elba, I shall soon be going away from you; and that parting will be painful to me, for I love you sincerely; but the idea of your welfare alleviates my regret, and, wherever I may be, I shall always be united to this island by the memory of the virtues of its inhabitants, and by my good wishes for them.

DALESME, General of Brigade.

Porto-Ferrajo, 4th May, 1814.

No. 9.

The new flag of the island, adopted by Napoleon, was immediately hoisted; and the fact was recorded in the following statement:—

ON this present 4th of May, 1814, his Majesty the Emperor Napoleon, having taken possession of the Island of Elba, General Drouot, Governor of the Island, in the name of Napoleon caused the flag of the island —a white ground, crossed diagonally by a red band with three golden bees—to be hoisted on the forts. This flag was saluted by the batteries of the forts on the coast, the English frigate, *Undaunted*, and the French vessels of war in the port. In witness whereof, we, Commissaries of the Allied Powers, have signed the above, together with General Drouot, Governor of the Island, and General Dalesme, Superior Commandant of the Island.

Done at Porto-Ferrajo, the 4th May, 1814.

[Here follow the signatures of the Commissaries.]

No. 10.

Two days after the date of the above document, the charge of the Vicar-General of the Island of Elba, Joseph-Philippe Arrighi, a distant relative of Napoleon, appeared.

JOSEPH-PHILIPPE ARRIGHI, Honorary Canon of the Cathedral of Pisa and the Metropolitan Church of Florence, etc. (under the Bishop of Ajaccio, Vicar-General of the Island of Elba and Principality of Piombino).

To our well-beloved in the Lord, our brethren composing the clergy, and to all the faithful of the island health and benediction!

Divine Providence, which, in its benevolence irre-

s

sistibly disposes all things, and assigns their destinies
to the nations, has decreed that, amid the political
changes of Europe, we should be the subjects of
Napoleon the Great.

The Island of Elba, already celebrated for its pro-
ducts, is about to become illustrious henceforth in
the history of nations through the homage which it
renders to its new Prince, whose glory is immortal.
The Island of Elba takes rank among nations, and its
narrow territory is ennobled by the name of its
Sovereign.

Elevated to so sublime an honour, it receives into
its bosom the Lord's anointed, and the other distinguished personages who accompany him.

When his Imperial and Royal Majesty made choice
of that island for his retreat, he made known to the
universe in what favour he held it!

What wealth is about to inundate our country!
What multitudes will flock from all sides to look
upon a hero!

The first day he set foot upon the shore, he proclaimed our destiny and our happiness.

"I will be a good father," said he; "be you my
cherished children."

Dear Catholics, what tender words! What expressions of kindness! What a pledge of our future
felicity! Let those words charm our thoughts, and
may they, being fixed in your minds, afford you an
inexhaustible source of consolation!

Let them be repeated by fathers to their children; let the remembrance of those words, by which the glory and the prosperity of the Island of Elba are secured, be perpetuated from generation to generation.

Fortunate inhabitants of Porto-Ferrajo, it is within these walls that the sacred person of his Imperial and Royal Majesty will dwell; among you, renowned in all times for the mildness of your character, and your affection for your Princes, Napoleon the Great will reside; never forget the favourable idea which he has formed of his faithful subjects.

And you, the faithful in Jesus Christ, conform yourselves to your destiny : "non sint schismata inter vos, pacem habeta, et Deus pacis et dilectionis erit vobiscum."

Let fidelity, gratitude, and submission reign in your hearts! Be you all united in respectful sentiments of love for your Prince, who is rather your father than your Sovereign. Celebrate with pious joy the goodness of the Lord, who, from all eternity, has reserved you to this happy event.

We command, in consequence, that next Sunday, in all the Churches, a solemn *Te Deum* shall be sung, in thanksgiving to the Almighty, for the favour which he has granted us in the abundance of His mercy.

Given at the Episcopal Palace of the Island of Elba, 6th of May, 1814.

ARRIGHI, Vicar-General.

FRANCESCO ANGIOLETTI, Secretary.

No. 11.

The two following letters furnish incontrovertible proof of Lucien's wish to go to the United States with his family, and of the negotiations which were set on foot between him and the English Cabinet with that object.

Neuilly, June 26, 1815.

You will have learned, my dear Pauline, the fresh misfortune that has befallen the Emperor, who has abdicated in favour of his son. He is about to depart for the United States, where we shall all join him. He is full of courage and calm. I shall endeavour to rejoin my family in Rome, in order to take them to America. If your health permit, we shall meet again there. Adieu, my dear sister. Mamma, Joseph, Jérôme, and I embrace you.

Your affectionate brother,

LUCIEN.

P.S.—I have retired to your pretty place at Neuilly.

————

No. 12.

A Letter from Cardinal Fesch to Princess Borghese.

Paris, June 29, 1815.

Lucien set out for London yesterday, in order to procure passports for the rest of his family.

Joseph will wait for his passports, Jérôme also. Lucien has left his second daughter, who has just arrived from England; she will return thither in a few days. I foresee that the United States will be the goal of these journeys. I think you ought to remain in Italy; but bear in mind that firmness of character is one of the most estimable gifts with which the Creator has endowed your family. Summon your courage, then, to imitate them in this, and place yourself above misfortune; nothing ought to hinder you from practising the closest economy. At present, we are all poor, even with what remains to us from last year.

Your mother and your brothers embrace you, and I do so likewise, with all my heart, with all the attachment which you know I feel.

Your affectionate Uncle,
CARDINAL FESCH.

A letter from the Bishop of Hortosia to M. de Talleyrand, Archbishop of Rheims, dated from Rome, the 15th of March, 1815, and which I give as a side light upon history, will elucidate the opinion which was professed by certain individuals among the high notabilities whom Napoleon had created during his reign, at the epoch of his return to France. This letter, which is not known, as it has never been printed, is a document of great value in the history of the Hundred Days.

s 3

My Lord,

The flight of Buonaparte is now known at Paris, and we learn that he was at Digne, in Provence, on the 24th of this month.

This flight has given us a more thorough knowledge of the men with whom we live. At first we perceived that there were many Jacobins at Rome, who were rejoiced at that flight, and spread the most absurd rumours; then came the English, ironically pretending to pity us, but afterwards talking of the great resources of Buonaparte and the number of malcontents in France; lastly, regarding him as already the master of the country.

Others said, " Why were not vessels of observation always there ? "

And when the reply was made, " But you had some there of your own, and you even had a Commissary in the island ? " " Yes," they would say; " but it was not our business to stop him."

" What, then, were you there for ? " said I, sharply, to the son of the famous Lord North, who passes for having a great deal of cleverness. " I can conceive that if you had seen Buonaparte, by himself, taking a sea-trip, you might have ignored it; but when you see a flotilla of seven vessels with fifteen hundred armed men and cavalry, the first duty of the ships which meet it is certainly to demand, Who are you, and whither are you going ? Acknowledge, sir, that you are to blame. Happily the philanthropic days of your sovereign Allies are past; it is for us to do justice upon him now. Confess that you are jealous of the revival of the prosperity of France?"

He answered not a word, and I changed the subject.

On the other hand, the Court of Rome regarded the Government of France as already changed. In his proclamations, Buonaparte again appeals to the liberty of the people.

His mother, who is still at Porto Ferrajo with Madame Bertrand, said to some English people who went to see her, that her son no longer fought to conquer; and, addressing the English, she added, " He will offer England an honourable peace."

These English are detestable! Almost all those who have come to Italy have been to see Buonaparte at Elba, and they even go there, now that he has left the island, to see his mother. Here, forty-six cases, sent by his mother, have been allowed to enter without inspection.

Cardinal Fesch said, yesterday, at the house of the Marchesa Massini, sister of the Duchesse d'Esclignac, that Buonaparte already had an army of fifty thousand men; that Masséna was for him, and that thirty departments had sent deputations to the Island of Elba, to invite him to France; he spoke in great delight. On all occasions this man shows that he is against the Bourbons; he is not worthy to be Archbishop of Lyons, and I am sure your Excellency will find a means of getting rid of him. He is an enemy

of the King; you should hear what his servants say
of him! In January, he refused the Ambassador's
invitation to attend the Mass at the church of St.
John Lateran, on Santa Lucia's day, in memory of
Henri IV. Although the Ambassador has behaved
too well to him, although he has asked him to dinner
twice, he has not deigned to visit him once. As for
me, I have not visited him, and even at the Ambassador's I have taken no notice of him.

Lucien, who, up to this moment, had appeared
indifferent about his brother, is now urging his cause.
The day before yesterday, at the house of the Princess
of Wales, who had just come from Naples, he talked
in the most unseemly way ; he laid out Buonaparte's
route, and told how he would be at Grenoble on the
6th, at Lyons on the 8th, and at Paris on the 15th,
adding that he must now have an army of eighty
thousand men.

This Princess of Wales is like a mad woman; she
is going away to-day without having seen Rome, and
she embarks at Ancona. Yesterday and the day
before, she had Cardinal Fesch and Lucien, one on her
right, the other on her left, all the evening ; and she
received only the English and some foreign Ministers,
not one French person was there. Besides, the Pope
has made it up with Murat; that is to say, he has
yielded and made a step backward. A month ago he
had the Post at Naples closed, and the letters taken
by force to the Papal Post. Since then, all communi-

cation was interrupted; but, the day before yesterday, we learned with astonishment that the Naples Post had been reopened. Your Excellency will see that France only obtains nothing. This is no doubt because we do not speak here with the firmness and dignity which becomes a great Power.

Lucien Buonaparte, Cardinal Fesch, Louis and Madame Buonaparte, are the zealous patrons of this Isoard, whom that cowardly Court would like to keep as judge-advocate of that of France. He is in constant correspondence with it, and is soliciting to be sent to Rome. His valet-de-chambre, who is expecting him, tells every one this. The Envoys Plenipotentiary of Austria and Spain obtain all that they demand, because they deal continually in threats.

What made the Pope yield to Murat? It was his having ordered his Consul to ask for his passports, and said, in a letter which he wrote to his Holiness, that he demanded passage for some troops. This, however, was refused, another route being indicated. It would not be inexpedient that his Majesty should be informed of all these matters.

This letter should have reached you, my Lord, earlier; but at the Legation they had not the goodness to give me notice that M. de Beaufrecourt was passing through, and would be for a week in Rome; for he dined at the Ambassador's, where I was not.

A thousand affectionate respects to your Excellency.

BISHOP OF HORTOSIA.

P.S.—The Pope has not replied to the letter of the Bishops, sent by Consalvi, because of your having signed it as the titulary of your See; otherwise it is favourably regarded.

THE END.